Bound by

Secrets

By: Kimberly Pryor

Copyright © 2024 All rights reserved.

None of this publication can be reproduced, copied in any format, by any means, electronic or otherwise, without prior consent from the publication and copyright owner.

This book is a work of fiction. Characters, names, places, and all incidents are from the author's mind and any resemblance of events or people is entirely coincidental.

Trigger Warning's

BDSM

Bondage

Torture

PTSD

Breath Play

Kidnapping

Psychological Abuse

Electric torture

Unaliving

Blood

Drugging

Humiliation

Violence

***Mental Health matters so if any of these triggers bother you this may not be the book for you and that is ok. Put you first. Optional mental health options below.**
*Call or text 988 or chat **988lifeline.org**.*

National Domestic Violence Hotline: 1-800-799-7233

Dedicated to all of my Lovely Lesbians and anyone else with a little darkness inside know your worth and never settle for less.

Chapter 1 (Sarah)

I have always felt like I was missing something in my life whether it was something missing or a void that was unfulfilled. Wait wait wait I am getting ahead of myself too much let me pump the breaks and go back a little and start from the beginning.

It all started on a hot summer day and the whole morning had gone wrong from the time I put my feet on the floor. You know that saying you got up on the wrong side of the bed, well if that was something that could be true it would have been true today.

I couldn't even get out the door good to go pick up all my supplies for the catering I was doing. I wanted to just get back in bed and try again another day, but I would not let anything ruin my day so let us get started.

My name is Sarah Lively, and I own Decadent Desire catering. I woke up late and as soon as my feet hit the floor it was a disaster. If disaster was a day today, was it. I live on the beach in a small cozy beach house away from the onslaught of tourists and noise but close enough that it was a hop skip and a jump to town.

I love waking up to the sounds of the waves crashing on the shore like she was angry at someone, and she wanted to rant and rave and be heard. The salt air was so thick you could taste it. I usually wake up and watch the sunrise on my patio while sipping on my caramel latte with a dash of marshmallowey goodness.

Today was not going to be that day. I overslept two hours because I have been having trouble sleeping, tossing, and turning all night trying to keep the nightmares at bay, but they were right there soon as my eyelids closed. I decided I was already late so I should just go ahead and stop by the Burnt Pelican which is the best coffee/tea shop in the area.

I go in and Andy is standing behind the counter, and he looks up as I walk in. Andy had this disheveled look about him but, it was all an act because he was one of the smartest people I have ever met. He was about 6'5 sun kissed skin as if the Sun Goddess herself kissed him, that is what you get living close to the ocean and he had sandy blonde hair with blue eyes. He hit the gym some, so he had a lean muscular body that the women went crazy over. He was the most eligible bachelor in town and all the women giggled like schoolgirls around him. I found it hilarious and especially when I was around all the women would shoot me dirty looks thinking I was trying to encroach on their territory. I laughed to myself all the time thinking in my head if they only knew I played for the same team.

There isn't anything like being with a woman. Everything about a woman is so enticing from the way a woman walks, to their lips and the curves of each individual woman's body. Um made me feel all tingly inside. Let me get back on track I can daydream about women all day. Andy has come to be one of my closest friends we hang out all the time. To be honest Andy is about the only friend I have. I have left my past life in a faraway place and never want to revisit it. I have a constant reminder in the ache of my hand every so often.

When I moved here it was a new chapter in my life, no let's just say a new book because I burnt the other one to ashes and started anew. My old life was full of monsters and demons but enough of that we aren't going to go down memory lane. When I started Decadent Desires, I put all my passion and hard work into it, and it was not easy to start over. I would sit in the Burnt Pelican Day after day. I sat there and had the best latte that the town had to offer. Andy was so nice and one day we just started talking about life. He asked me what I did for work, and I gave him one of my business cards. I cater and do private dinners. I have always loved food and been one hell of a cook. I put love and seasoning into every delicious bite. I have a way with food that will give your tastebuds a sense of euphoria.

Andy helped me get new clients and the biggest client I was to have yet is the one I was running late to. I walked in and he said "Well looky looky who just rolled out of bed."

Chuckling and handing me my caramel drizzled latte. I could feel the daggers from the couple of women standing at the counter enough to make me shiver. I turned to them and fained a stab to my heart as I turned back around rolling my eyes, I took one whiff of my latte, and it instantly calmed me. I stopped and inhaled the scent of marshmellowy goodness closing my eyes to fully appreciate the smell of deliciousness.

Andy brought me back to reality by pulling my arm and guiding me to the deck that overlooked the ocean. The heat and salt air hit us as we walked out into the sun, and it almost blinded me. I stood there trying to let my eyes readjust to the sun hearing the waves crash onto the shore. As I sipped the latte, I smiled.

"I thought those women were going to stab me because if looks could kill I would have been dead one hundred times over your fan club is getting ruthless" I chuckled.

Andy laughed and sat down. We sit there taking in the air and relaxing. Andy leaned into me and said, "Sarah you must be on your A game tonight."

I blinked and turned toward him and said "I always am."

"Yes, you are, but this is different. I told you Lavonna holds a lot of authority in this town. Tonight, can make or break you." Andy replied.

We were standing by the end of the deck when I heard this voice come from behind us. The voice was like velvet rubbing against your skin. Her voice was one when she spoke you did not question it. I didn't know whether it enticed me or made my blood run cold. It made my heart skip a beat for a second and I had no idea why. She was speaking with Andy when I heard my name.

"Sarah earth to Sarah …..." Andy called.

I turned startled, almost spilling my drink. I blinked up at them both like I was coming out of a daze.

Andy steadied me and said "Sarah, I want you to meet Lavonna Black."

I was taken aback as I gazed up into her mahogany brown eyes and it was like I was falling into them. I regained myself and I scolded myself in my head. She was the most gorgeous woman I had ever seen. She had on this black pantsuit that was most definitely tailored just for her because it hugged every curve, not too feminine but not too masculine either but, in a way that you could tell she gets what she wants. I looked at her and her demeanor exuded dominance. She smiled and when she did it was intoxicating like a moth to a flame and for a moment, I thought I was the moth. She reached out her hand and I put my hand in hers, it was like electricity ran through my body, she had a firm grip and shook hands well.

She smiled and said "I have heard spectacular things and am looking forward to it. I can't wait to taste whatever is on the menu for tonight."

Thinking to myself I sure as fuck wish I were on the menu. Shaking that thought out of my head and telling myself to get my mind out of the gutter.

I smiled and replied, "The meal will leave you desiring more."

I see her cock an eyebrow.

"Well in that case I am in the mood for a little desire."

Heat flushed up my face and I couldn't stop it. She just acted like it never happened and waved bye to me and Andy and walked out.

I watched as she slid her Sunglasses back on and glided out of the room as she disappeared through the coffee shops doors. Watching her walk out was definitely a great view. I heard Andy clearing his throat with a slight chuckle.

"What was that about? You could cut the sexual tension with a knife between you two."

"Haha" I scoffed at him and punched him ever so friendly in the shoulder.

"You know I am not ready for any of that" even though my body was aching just from that small touch of when we shook hands.

I need to get laid but, to be honest my desires ran a little dark and it is not easy finding someone that wants to play in the dark with you. I said my goodbyes to Andy and headed to the local farmer's market.

I loved getting the freshest ingredients and the people of this town were so nice. Since this is a dinner for two, I wanted it to be the best dinner I have cooked so far. Lavonna wanted the full shebang, and she would have it. The appetizer being homemade spring rolls with a sauce that was a little sweet but, when it hits your palette dissolves into a little spice that clings to your tongue. I will serve small, chilled Caesar salads as I am making the entrée. As for the entrée I am going with Peppered Bacon wrapped filets special cuts from Ted the hometown butcher. I am making rose shaped potatoes with sauteed broccolini. Then comes dessert which will be two small individual funnel cakes with a chocolate covered strawberry on top with a side of ice cream with a drizzle of caramel and chocolate.

I was wondering who Lavonna's plus one was going to be. I was running so late because I had to stop by the butchers and the printing shop to pick up the menus for the night and stop by the florist for the flowers for the arrangement. Lavonna had spared no expense for this night. I was given the address and specific instructions to be let in early to set up everything and have everything ready by the time they were done with their meeting. It seemed like time flew by as I was running all the errands and going from store to store, I looked at my watch and realized that time was continuously running.

Damn it I said to myself as I placed the address into my gps. Where would we be these days without gps I do not miss the maps and having to figure out the roads not listed. Pulling up to the gated fence I pressed the button that would signal to the security. An elderly gentleman came over the intercom asking me to state my business. I gave them my name and

 he said, "oh you're the caterer."

"Yes" I replied.

A moment later the big wrought iron gates started to open. The gates were massive, and they were intricately designed being total black with one woman on one side and another woman on the other side. When closed it looked like they were reaching out for one another and while they were opening it was like they were ushering you in. I slowly drove my black Toyota Rav 4 through the gate while admiring the whole effect of the gate.

The landscaping was gorgeous, and I drove up the winding driveway to the house. Weeping willows stood on both sides of the road. As I drove up to the house my mouth dropped this place was to die for. The house was like a fairy tale it was a two-story Victorian home with a beautiful fountain in the front with two naked women in an embrace. I started to sense the theme and wondered if Ms. Lavonna played for the same team I did. I could see that something about her screamed Lesbian but these days you can't just assume. The brick was laid with black, and gold as well had a marble staircase leading up to the front door. The columns looked like they were made from pure gold as it shined off the marble staircase.

I rang the doorbell and a young Hispanic woman mid-thirties with chocolate brown eyes and a very warm smile. Behind that smile, you knew she was wise beyond her years and had seen her share of rough times but never stopped going. She ushered me in and had someone help me with all the bags and showed me to the kitchen.

I was amazed how big the kitchen was and almost made me want to cry. I have always wanted a kitchen like this. No expense was spared from the double stainless-steel ovens in the wall to the marbled countertops but, we are not here for me to have a moment over a kitchen.

I got to work taking everything out of the bags I had counterspace for days. I wanted to get organized and figure out where I wanted to start first. The first thing was to get the table, and the decorations set up. I still wondered who would be sitting across from Lavonna and I felt a ping of jealousy.

Where the hell had that come from, I don't even know this woman and why was I feeling jealous?

I quelled that feeling, shaking it off laughing at myself.

I needed to get my pussy licked soon because this was not like me. I was walking to the dining room and was fumbling with the red and black roses in my hand. The black roses had to be special ordered when I ran straight into Lavonna. She grabbed my hand and caught me at my waist, and we ended up against a wall with her face right beside mine. My heart skipped a beat, and it was like all the oxygen had left the room.

"Are you ok?" she asked.

She still had me pressed up against the wall and one hand around my waist and the other one holding my hand. When I could finally take a breath, I smelled the scent of her cologne it was faint and mixed in with the scent of coconut. She smiled up at me from inches apart. Her voice slid along my skin rubbing in places a voice cannot rub.

I gazed into her chocolate brown eyes almost losing myself.

I blinked and stammered out "Yes I am ok; I am so sorry I wasn't paying attention to where I was going."

The red and black roses lay scattered around our feet.

She looked down and she said, "you are bleeding."

I must have pricked my hand on one of the thorns of the roses. She lifted my hand, and I was still against the wall. She let go of my waist and put her hand on the wall. I wanted to sink into the wall at this very moment.

Why did this woman undo me so?

She was looking at the blood on my finger as if she were pondering something. She then lifted my finger to her lips and all I could do was watch her watching me as she put my finger to those luscious pink lips and licked the blood from my finger. I thought I would faint right there, and I shook whatever hold she had on me and pulled my hand from her lips.

"Ms. Black, I need to get back to work." I choked out.

She cocked her head and moved back.

"Of course."

I started walking away as I heard her say.

"Sarah, aren't you forgetting something?"

I was stopped in my tracks knowing I had left all the roses on the floor. I was just so ready to get as far away as I could. I turned back.

"Yes, I am so sorry."

I walked and knelt in front of her to pick up the roses that were laying at her feet. She stood there staring down at me. She then knelt and picked up a few that were remaining on the floor while looking at me in the eyes.

What was with her?

As she was staring this woman's confidence was off the charts. I started getting angry at myself for letting this woman rattle me so.

"Here you go."

She reached out with her hand full of roses. I had to stop my hand trembling so as I took them from her, and she glided her hand across mine. Lavonna got up and started walking away but as she walked away, she stopped, and I was still kneeling on the floor.

"I get what I want Ms. Lively, and I need for you to remember that" and with that she walked out.

What in the actual fuck did she mean by that?

When I walked back into the kitchen there was a band aid lying next to my things. The rest of the night flew by. Everything went flawlessly. After serving the dessert and heading back to the kitchen I was so thrilled and bummed all at the same time.

The woman that Lavonna was sitting across from was built like a model and she was dripping sex appeal. She is tall and thin with gorgeous legs for days. Her skin was sun kissed. Long black hair that shined in the light like looking at black diamonds. Piercing blue eyes that was like the purest blue sky before a huge storm rolled in.

I cannot measure up to that. I am not ugly by any means and when I step out baby I can step out. I am 5'6 with thick thighs and top heavy with some extra cushion to hold onto. I shook the thought from my head and started cleaning everything up.

I put my earphones in and was listening to some classic R&B. As, I was putting everything that I brought into the bags and was getting ready to walk out the door Lavonna comes in the door with an envelope. My breath caught and I scowled at myself.

I will not let this woman think she has any type of effect on me.

I was telling myself that as my pussy was betraying me and started to slowly drip down my thighs and that made me scowl even harder. Lavonna noticed and asked,

"Is there something wrong Sarah?"

I shook myself and readjusted my face.

"I was just thinking about some things I had to do while I was walking out."

I apologized to her and in my head.

Why the fuck are you apologizing to this woman you have done nothing wrong? I wondered.

"Let me walk you out."

Before I could say no, she grabbed one of the bags from my hand and started walking to the door. I stood there for a second then headed for the door with her. We walked in silence to the car. When we made it to the car, I opened the trunk and placed my bag in the trunk and reached for the bag that Lavonna was holding, and it was like she didn't want to let go and when she did her fingers slid over mine like a painter's first brushstroke.

I closed my eyes for a split second and regained my composer as my anger rose to the top. Letting myself hold on to that because this woman will not be my undoing. I kept my face neutral.

"Is there anything else Ms. Black?"

My tone came out short and clipped even to me there was a moment of shock but just for an instant then her face slid into that perfect neutral face that said everything and nothing at the same time. She reached out and gave me the envelope.

"Are you booked for tomorrow?"

"No, I am not" I replied.

"Can I procure your services tomorrow as well, but a vegan style dish?"

"Yes, I can manage that," and she turned and walked off.

I drove and looked at the envelope in my passenger seat and it was even sealed with a gorgeous black wax seal. I didn't know whether to keep my anger or was I just overreacting. My emotions were all over the place as I pulled in my driveway.

I got out as I usually do, and something stopped me in my tracks. I got this sensation like ice running down my spine. Something was off. I keep a Beretta BU9 Nano in my console and I didn't know if I was going to be able to reach it in time, but nothing was happening. I stood there still, with that eerie feeling crawling up my neck I slowly looked around and couldn't see anything out of the ordinary, but knew something wasn't right. I grabbed my keys and started walking fast to the door.

I installed the locks that had to have the fingerprint sensor on, and I glanced back trying to not show I was unnerved. I put my finger on the lock, and I heard the whine of the lock give. I pushed the door and almost collapsed on the floor. Slamming the door and locking it sinking down to the floor in tears and thought to myself.

This cannot be happening again.

Chapter 2 (Sarah)

I rolled over and fumbled for my phone to turn the piercing sound of the alarm off. My head was throbbing and felt like I had just walked through hell and back. I lay there still shaken about last night.

After having hysteria at the door, I calmed myself enough to try to take a relaxing hot bath. The bath didn't relax me, but I knew I had to get up and go on with my life. I cannot step back into that space of always looking over my shoulder and being scared.

On the side of the bed, I stared at my custom red and black Smith & Wesson 9mm in its holster. I knew it was time to hit the range again to ease some of this tension.

Now I know that everyone is thinking and wondering what is going on. Well, that is my past trying to come into my present and I sure as *hell* won't let that happen.

I groaned as my feet hit the floor because my body felt like I was someone's punching bag for the night. I tossed and turned at every noise. From the angry groaning of the sea which I usually welcomed but it has recently become something that unnerved me. I stood looking in the mirror at my long red disheveled hair and said,

"Sarah get a *fucking* grip."

I closed my eyes, breathed in and out and releasing all the tension that was in my shoulders. I looked in the mirror and the woman that was staring back at me looked like she was ready for anything.

I got dressed and walked out the door. I was in my car and taking in all the heat when I remembered the white envelope Lavonna gave me last night. Immediately looking over and it was still lying on the seat where I had placed it. I don't know what I was expecting but my mouth suddenly became dry. I was scared to open it. I needed coffee so I started my car and headed to see Andy at the Burnt Pelican.

On the drive, I was mulling in my head if some secrets needed to stay buried or if I needed to trust Andy because we have been friends for a while. I pulled around back where Andy parked his Jeep and yes, he had the stereotypical jeep with the top and the doors off to enjoy the beach life.

I grabbed the envelope from the passenger side and headed in through the employee entrance. I was on my way to open Andy's office door when I heard voices; damn he was in a meeting. I knew who he was meeting with because only one woman's voice had ever caught my breath and felt like smooth velvet against my skin. I may need to investigate vampires because no one person should have this sort of effect on another human being. I could hear them whispering but couldn't make out what they were saying. Of course, red flags went up.

What have I gotten myself into?

I was still on edge and knew I was jumping to conclusions. I remembered the envelope in my hand and quickly put it in my purse. I was pulling my hand out of my purse when the doors to the office opened. Here I was, staring into Lavonna Black's drowning pool of brown eyes. Standing this close I could see that her eyes were deep brown tapered into a caramel like your favorite coffee with a little added creamer to make it sweeter.

"Well, hello again Ms. Lively, if we keep running into one another, I am going to have to call it fate."

"Fate huh, maybe one could call it coincidence." I rolled my eyes.

I really don't know why I was being so cross at her. Maybe because of the way my body reacted to her, it was like a betrayal. She cocked an eyebrow and was about to say something when Andy cleared his throat and stepped up.

"Good morning, Sarah, I will be with you in a sec after I walk Lavonna out."

Lavonna spoke without looking back and said, "no bother Andy go make Sarah her usual Carmel latte with a little bit of marshmallow crème."

I could not hide the shock on my face as she just walked out the door and left me staring at Andy.

"Before you say anything, let me make you a latte and meet you outside."

He must have known that he was fixing to get an earful. As I was walking through the bustling little coffee shop the aroma hit me full force. I walked out of the Employees Only door and up the spiral staircase that opened to a small balcony that looked over the ocean.

Sitting down in the plush rocking chair and began to ponder if Andy was really my friend, who the hell is this mysterious Lavonna, and what the fuck were they just whispering about in his office. By now my mind was going ninety to nothing. Why hadn't I seen Lavonna in his office until now? I sat in the chair looking out at the sea wondering what I should do.

I heard the door open and watched Andy come through with two glasses. As he came closer, I started to wonder if I really knew Andy or was that me just overthinking everything because I was on edge. My ponderance must have shown because he sighed, sat down and gave me the cup. The cup was warm when he placed it in my hand, it smelt good, but I suddenly felt a chill in my bones. I sat the cup down and looked at Andy. He held his hand up and before I could utter a word, he said.

"Let me explain and everything will make sense. First, Lavonna asked about what you choose to drink because it smelled heavenly. It was innocent enough, so I told her. I couldn't have known that she was going to bring it up like that. It seems that you Sarah Lively have rattled and caught the attention of Lavonna Black and that is rare very rare indeed."

I looked out at the sea.

"Why haven't I seen her here before and now it is like she is here all the time? Andy, I heard y'all whispering in the office."

"Oh, is that why you are so stand offish and haven't even taken a drink of your latte yet. Well, if you must know, we were discussing business. Lavonna is my silent partner and has always been. She comes around ever so often, but she is always busy doing something. Lavonna Black has helped every business around here; one way or another. We went to school together and have always been friends."

"Has she always been this........?" As I was looking for the right word to use.

"Yes, she has always been this intense. She has always made sure she has gotten everything she wants."

"I guess that makes sense." I replied.

I fumbled through my bag looking for the envelope she had given me and sat it on the table. Andy's eyebrow raised.

"Did she give you that?"

"Yes, last night. I was going to open it when I made it home, but I had somewhat of a scare."

Andy reached for the envelope but stopped in mid motion and let his hand fall back to the side.

"Sarah, what happened? I have trusted you with information that no one in this town knows but if we are being honest with one another, it is you who is the mystery. Sarah, you showed up one day out of nowhere. No family, no pets, no past. I have never asked because I figured you would tell me when you got ready."

"I don't owe you an explanation for anything," I said in anger.

I immediately regretted it as I caught his arm as he rose from his chair.

"I am sorry Andy you didn't deserve that. I am scared and angry, but I shouldn't have taken that out on you. Come to the house when you can, and I will tell you everything and then you will know my secrets."

Chapter 3(Sarah)

I was in my own world driving home letting the salty air hit my face completely lost in thought. Have you ever wondered when you come out of thought how you made it to anywhere driving. I jolted out of my head and almost missed my turn to the house. I slowed and pulled down my drive and could hear the waves crashing angerly into the shore. I looked up at the sky and knew there was a storm brewing, and the sea knew it. Closing my eyes, breathing in, and letting the sounds of the waves hit my ears. I smiled to myself and let my stress fade away on the waves.

I walked to the door, as I was putting the key in the lock, not using the fingerprint entry. Goosebumps suddenly inched up my spine. My hand started shaking and the key slid from my hand and bounced on the wooden porch. While reaching down to pick up the key at the moment the sky opened, lightning flashed, and thunder pierced my ears. I let out a little yelp. I laughed to myself, picked up the key, and let myself into the house. My hands were full, so I walked over and put my purse and bags on the counter. The envelope from Lavonna slipped out of my purse. I stopped and stared at it when I heard my phone ding. I checked my phone and realized it was my camera out front letting me know someone was at the door. I figured it was Andy because he has a key.

I went to make some good ole sweet tea as the door started to open. I turned with the kettle in my hand and was frozen with fear as I saw a slender manicured hand slipping through the door. All I felt was fear and I wanted to scream but no sound came out. She was standing there wearing a long black hoodie and I was frozen at that moment. I watched as the kettle fell and shattered at my feet. All I could do was stare at the brown eyes that were staring back at me. If you looked closely there was gold that circled the irises that made you think of the deepest golden sunflowers. I finally started screaming and I couldn't quit. That was the last thing I remembered before everything went dark.

I awoke laying in my bed with Lavonna's hand on my forehead. I squealed; Andy came running to my side. Lavonna stood and let Andy in my view. He started to scream my name. I eventually came to myself as he had his hands on the sides of my shoulders. Through cries, muddled screams, and tear-stained hair, I could see Lavonna. My sobs slowed and all I could see was her sitting in the chair at the end of the bed watching me intensely. The look in her eyes I couldn't make out, it was almost demonic. When she noticed that I was watching her expression, she changed to that unreadable oozing sex appeal that she wore for her blank face. She got up and walked towards us. I had forgotten that Andy was still holding me. I sniffed, Andy got up and told me he would be right back. I reached out to him and before I could say anything.

"Everything is ok now. I will be right back. Lavonna will stay with you while I go put on coffee and get you a hot towel."

Lavonna slowly sat on the bed but kept her distance. She looked off and said,

"Silence should never be awkward and sometimes it is all that is needed."

So, we sat in silence. That was more comforting than anything I have ever experienced. I sat there feeling so vulnerable, my tear-stained face, my hair stuck to it from all the crying. I saw Lavonna reach out, pick the hair from my face, and place it behind my ear. I recoiled from her touch. Leaving her hand hanging in the balance. She took back her hand as Andy came walking in with a tray. She got up and as she was walking out, she said with her back to us,

"I have a meeting I must attend and then a dinner date later but if Ms. Lively cannot make it tonight, I will understand."

Before I could think, I answered "I will be there, Ms. Black."

She nodded "I will see myself out."

I watched Andy put down the tray on the bedside table. He gave me a hot towel and it felt so good to let the warmth of the towel soothe my skin and calm me. I felt the bed give way to him sitting down on it, my face buried in the hot towel.

Andy whispered, "are you ok?"

I took a deep breath in and looked at him.

"Yes, I will be."

He started with hesitation.

"Do you know the person that ran away as we pulled up?"

Fear and shock shook me and all I could do was stare at the damp cold towel now in my hands. He grabbed me by the shoulders and shook me. I looked at him colorless with horror on my face. All I could say in a hushed whisper was that she had found me, she actually found me. Andy sat on the floor peering up into my face.

"Who found you Sarah?"

I breathed and closed my eyes and chased the bile that had been building at the back of my throat down. I focused on my breathing for what seemed like ages, but I knew it was only a few minutes. I slowed my breathing, opened my eyes, and looked at Andy. Reaching for the lukewarm espresso Andy had made and took in the scent as it calmed me a little. Andy stared at me just waiting for me to say anything. You would have been able to hear a pin drop at that moment. I studied Andy and his disheveled look told me he cared about me. I smiled at him, and I could feel the wave of relief and tension ease out of him like the waves receding from the tide. He got up and pulled the chair Lavonna had been sitting in closer to the bed. I asked him what he had saw and we would start from there. In this moment I decided that I would explain everything.

"Lavonna forgot to give you the list of things for tonight and she wanted to drop it by and since it was on the way she followed me here. As we were walking up to the door talking, we heard screams, and your door was ajar. We ran inside and there was a hooded person standing over you. They ran out onto your balcony, and I ran after them. Damn, I must be out of shape because I lost them. I am so sorry Sarah. I came back to the house and Lavonna had laid you on the bed and was fixing to call the ambulance when you started to come too. I told her that you didn't like hospitals, she was annoyed but at least she didn't call them. Also, we found this lying next to you."

He raised a necklace that held one solitary sunflower etched in gold with a black diamond in the middle. I gasped and recoiled like a child from something that just burned them. I breathed in and I scolded myself, you can't let her get the best of you. I slowly reached for the necklace, and it was as time stood still. I felt cold and when I looked at the necklace, I knew it was Jade.

I told Andy about how I had gotten home and must have forgotten to lock the door and thought it was him coming in. When I turned, Jade was the one coming in. I must have fainted and gone down hard because when I came to, I had a headache. Thankfully, I didn't fall on any of the glass that had shattered when the kettle hit the ground. I finally sighed and let all the stress out. There was a definite stress along my shoulders that I really felt now.

"Thank you" I whispered.

Also, made a mental note to thank Lavonna for today. Looking at the clock I realized how late dinner for Lavonna was going to be. I started thanking myself for shopping earlier in the day for what I needed. Jumping up, my head ached a little, but I couldn't miss out on this money, it would pay my bills for at least the next month.

Andy told me to slow down and think if I really wanted to go cook and set up after today's events. He also reminded me that I hadn't told him who Jade was yet. I stopped, sighed, and looked at him.

"She stole five years of my life, and I refuse to let her steal any more time."

"OKAY one condition; I drive you to Lavonna's and you tell me about Jade."

I sighed, "I owe you at least that."

If I was really being honest with myself, I was kind of relieved I didn't have to drive both to Lavonna's and home alone tonight. I told him that he would have to get me after dinner and he said,

"Of course, what do you expect to walk home" we both laughed.

So, it takes about thirty minutes to get to Lavonna's house from mine. I sat on the passenger side of Andy's jeep and started to give him the reader's digest version of mine and Jades history; it wasn't pretty. I hid nothing from Andy as we drove to

Lavonna's. I told him everything from mental and physical abuse, stalking, and threats. I kept it short, sweet, and didn't go into the details. I told him if he wanted to know more, I would tell him. He pulled up to Lavonna's and helped me carry everything into the kitchen.

This kitchen still amazed me every time I walked into it. It was a dream come true for those who like to cook. I told him to just lay everything down and I would get the rest. He told me that he was going to find Lavonna; speak, and that he would be back to pick me up later tonight. Andy told me to just shoot him a text when I was almost done so I wouldn't have to wait on him to get here.

I found myself letting go of what had happened today while I was preparing and getting everything ready for tonight. If you haven't guessed, cooking was my happy place. I was setting up the table and placing the red and white tulips in the vase when Lavonna came in the door. I looked up and was about to thank her when Luna (the maid) walked in and told Lavonna her guest had arrived. I hadn't learned her name the night before but, I made it a point to ask today. My Spanish was a little rusty, but she grinned and patted my hand, nonetheless. She had such a warm smile. She was around my age, but she acted like she was so much older.

This night was like the last but there was a new woman sitting across from Lavonna. Now this woman was still gorgeous, but she was opposite of the woman from last night. This made me wonder about Lavonna. The woman looked like she had just walked out of an Egyptian fantasy. Her skin was like water at night so still and flawless and the gold jewelry that she wore gleamed off her gorgeous skin. Where the hell did, she find these women. They were a wet dream come to life and they purred like a cat in heat for Lavonna. I could understand their emotions, but damn, why did this get under my skin. I guess money does get you whoever you want.

It's not like she needed it with the looks and charisma that just oozed out of every perfect pore in her body. Lavonna herself was a wet dream come true. Caramel skin, with long black straightened hair every suit was tailored to fit her in the right places. She smelled of honeysuckle and coconut. She commanded the attention of the whole room. Dominance hit you like a tidal wave. I have always been a sucker for dominance.

I scoffed at myself and shook myself out of my thoughts. Dinner went well, I had almost forgotten to text Andy. I was picking up my phone when Lavonna walked into the kitchen. I jumped a little because I don't know why this woman just unnerved me so much. I was drawn to her in some way so maybe I was mad at myself.

"There you go with that scowl on your face again, if I didn't know any better, I would say you don't like me, Ms. Lively."

Her eyebrow raised as she stared at me waiting for an answer. To be honest, I didn't know what to tell her because I didn't make a habit of lying to someone, but she was paying me pretty good. So, I settled on the half-truth and answered.

"You puzzle me Ms. Black."

I shrugged, looked at her and then turned away to let Andy know that I would be done soon, and he could start to head my way. As I hit send, I realized Lavonna was still there. As I looked towards her, she pushed off from the counter and started walking toward me. Again, my body started to betray me. My heart picked up its pace and my mouth was suddenly dry. I couldn't swallow as she came over to me. Lavonna looked at me.

"Since recent events, I have decided that you will stay here at least tonight, and we will see how everything goes tomorrow."

My mouth fell open and at that the scowl was back on my face.

"You decided huh?"

She smirked "You don't approve?"

I scoffed, "I have my very own place I don't need to stay here."

I was pissed and I felt betrayed by Andy. Did he tell her about Jade? Did he tell her my dark secrets. She laughed and raised her eyebrow; it pissed me off even more.

"Before you start being pissy at Andy, he told me nothing. I did ask but he was like a rock. We both agreed on you staying here for the night, since you are without a way to get home."

Shit, shit, shit, I cursed to myself and still cursed Andy. I looked at Lavonna and said "no." I picked up my purse and started to walk to the front door. When I placed my hand on the doorknob to open it a hand pushed the door shut. I whipped around to give Lavonna a piece of my mind but here she was staring straight into my eyes. It was like staring into a predator's eyes and I was the prey. Her voice walked slowly along my skin, she whispered but it was like she was yelling. It was only a whisper.

"This is, not up for negotiation and Ms. Lively I get what I want."

My breath caught in my throat. I wanted to react so bad but, deep down I felt safe here even though the look in her eyes were wild. I don't know if it excited me, or if it was fear, but I also felt relief. I didn't want to be at the house alone tonight, but I was stubborn and prideful.

My phone beeped; it was a message from Andy. I looked down, still aware that Lavonna had not moved. I read the message.

Please forgive me I know you are probably mad, but I would rather have you mad and safe than not safe. Sarah, Lavonna has security just stay with her one night and if it bugs you, I will come and get you tomorrow. I trust Lavonna with my life.

I sighed, all the events of the day had come crashing down on me and exhaustion set in. I looked into Lavonna's eyes.

"Fine only for one night."

She gave me that smirk and eased away from me and called for Luna. She appeared out of nowhere.

"Show Ms. Lively to her room for the night."

As she was walking away

"I told you I always get what I want when it comes to what is mine."

What in the actual fuck did she mean by that? I was too tired to contemplate her riddles tonight. Luna led me upstairs to the end of the hall and opened the door and told me if I needed anything don't hesitate to ask. I assured her I didn't need anything and to have a good night.

She smiled "Buenos Noches (Goodnight) Ms. Lively" and shut the door behind her.

I was left staring at this magnificent, lavish room. My eyes couldn't take it all in. I slowly walked around the room to the dimly lit fireplace which was on for the light. It wasn't giving off any heat because it was the middle of the summer. The flames were dancing over my skin and the wall. I walked over to the huge king-sized bed and there on the bed lay a gorgeous blood red robe and a set of black satin pjs.

How did she know these are my favorite colors? Where did Lavonna get these and how was everything my size?

I shrugged suddenly as I felt the stress of the day hit me like a ton of bricks. I just wanted to take a bath and crawl into bed. I walked into the bathroom and my chin hit the floor like one of those old cartoons. There was blackened marble everywhere and in the middle was the biggest jacuzzi tub I have ever seen. On the wall was a huge two head shower and to the right was the walk-in closet with a vanity I would have killed for.

I wanted a bath so bad, but I was mentally and physically exhausted. I let out a sigh as I passed up the opportunity to soak in this gorgeous tub. Being so tired, I probably would have drowned myself. I could hear the news now; catering woman drowned in Millionaires house, was it a coincidence?

I walked to the shower and got undressed. I turned on the water and let the steam start to rise. I liked the water to burn me to my soul and I just stood under the cascading rain type showerhead and just let the stress wash down the drain. I had left the bathroom door ajar, and I thought I heard knocking. I eased my head out of the water and listened and then I heard Lavonna's voice calling my name. Then there was a knock on the door. My breath caught and I had to clench my thighs together because she, as in my pussy, was trying to betray me. Damn, it was starting to tingle down there. I shook it off and I replied.

"I will be out in a second."

Lavonna called back to me and told me to take my time and when I finished showering there was a toothbrush and toothpaste in a bag on the counter for me.

I brushed my teeth and slipped into satin pajamas. They fit like a glove except in the chest area I had Double D's, and they were kina spilling out. My nipples were showing through the satin and the rings in my nipples were plain to see but to be honest most of the time I was at home I slept nude. With the thought of home, a scowl crept on my face. Jade invaded my sanctuary and my peace.

I was towel drying my hair as I walked into the room. Lavonna was sitting on the loveseat lounging, staring into the fire. As I walked in her gaze turned to me and her eyes started at the top of my head and walked their way down my body. I could feel my skin start to flush and it wasn't because I had just gotten out of the shower. She slowly got up and started walking toward me, her eyes never leaving mine. I instantly backed up and hit the bed. I must have hit the bed hard because I ended up sitting on it. I could hear my heartbeat in my ears, it was so loud. She picked up the mug of hot chocolate from the bedside table, and she was so close her pjs were slightly touching me. She smelled like honeysuckle and coconut. She handed me the hot chocolate and not surprising it had small marshmallows in it.

"Ms. Lively, I wanted to check on you and bring you some hot chocolate before bed."

I peered up at her as she was standing over me. I was sitting on the edge of the bed, reaching out and hating that my hand was shaking but Ms. Black never said a word. She unnerved me and turned me on at the same damn time. I shook out of it and took the cup from her hands. Her fingers grazed mine and it was like electricity ran where she had touched. I had a frown on my face.

"What is wrong Ms. Lively, there you go again making me think you do not like me?"

With the scowl present on my face. "I appreciate the hospitality but, you did not have to let me stay here."

"Well, it was either you stay with me, or Andy and it was no sense in him coming all the way here to get you when I have plenty of room."

"I appreciate it but….."she placed a finger over my lips.

"No buts just get some rest and you are free to go tomorrow."

I clicked my tongue, I didn't say anything, but her eyebrow raised, and she started walking to the door.

"If you need anything …..anything at all my room is at the end of the hall."

"Thank you but I believe I will be just fine."

Chapter 4(Sarah)

Lavonna walked out and shut the door behind her. I sat there holding the cup of hot chocolate. It was just how I liked it, not surprising to me. It warmed my hands with the sudden chill I had just gotten. I sipped, and it was an amazing hint of creamy smores with marshmallow cream. I sat the cup on the saucer on the bedside and slipped between the covers while the bed enveloped me. I never knew a bed could feel so good.

I lay there watching the flames dancing on the walls till I drifted off to sleep. My night was riddled with nightmares; I tossed and turned all night. I could have sworn that I had woken myself up and saw Lavonna sitting in the chair. I was so tired I figured I was imagining things. Finally, my sleep was deep enough that I was able to rest. But in my sleep, I was right back to my nightmares. It was like I couldn't breathe, and I kept screaming but nothing would come out. Suddenly, I was shaken awake. Everything was like coming out of a fog. Lavonna was there holding my arms down and saying my name and telling me to wake up. Her hair was a mess, and she looked as disheveled as I felt. It was worry in her eyes and then in a fleeting moment it was that lovely face she always wore. I started weeping. She slowly sat on the bed and brought me to her and just held me. I was too tired to protest, I just cradled into her weeping uncontrollably. She sat there running her hands through my hair quietly singing in my ear and telling me that it was going to be alright. My sobs had ceased, and I was listening to that velvety voice when it hit me where I was and whose arms I was in. I groaned to myself and quickly moved back on the bed. My tear-stained face lifted apologizing to Lavonna for all that had happened through the night. Her pajamas were soaked from my tears.

This had to be the most embarrassing moment in my life. She looked at me.

"Are you ok?"

All I could do was nod. She spoke to me like you would speak to a scared child.

"I am going to get you a warm towel."

She slowly got up, she showed me her hands and walked into the bathroom. The light switched on and I heard water running. I heard the water stop as I was sitting on the bed with my arms wrapped around my legs. *Who was I? Why is this getting to me so bad?* In that moment Jades image flashed in front of my eyes. Lavonna was back sitting on the bed and slowly reaching for my face. I stilled like she was going to slap me. She stopped and, in that voice, she said.

"Everything is fine, and I am only going to wipe your face."

The towel felt good against my skin. I gave her a weak smile and mumbled out a "Thank you."

I looked at her as she sat on the bed and I kind of half snorted/giggled to myself.

"Well, this makes twice in one day you have saved me from my tears and comforted me."

Lavonna smiled, leaned in and whispered,

"Ms. Lively, you can make it up to me anytime."

My face went flush, and I couldn't get a syllable out. Oh, how I wish I could buy a vowel but couldn't think of anything to say to save my life, so I just looked away.

"Oh, I see no comeback well I guess the cats got your tongue."

For a split second everything was gone, and I murmured "I wish your tongue was on my cat." I thought that I was low enough she couldn't hear it.

"What did you say Ms. Lively?"

I perked up.

"I just wanted to thank you for everything."

There was a sinister smirk on Lavonna's face as she went into the bathroom. She came out in a black tank top and her pajama pants. She walked around the bed and started climbing in; my heart was suddenly in my throat. I couldn't hear anything over the ringing in my ears. My voice was panting and stumbling,

"What are you doing Ms. Black?"

"What does it look like I am doing I am going to lay down and get some sleep."

"But don't you have a room and a bed to go to?"

"This one is just fine," and she turned her back to me and laid down.

I was still sitting up and it was as if she knew I was still staring at her. I was staring like she had sprouted three heads.

"Lay down Sarah, morning will come soon, and you need some sleep."

I opened my mouth to say something.

"This is not up for negotiation."

I slowly laid down rigid as a board. I lay there not knowing what to think because I could feel her warmth. This woman scared me and made my breath quicken all at the same time. I did feel safer with her in bed though. I finally closed my eyes and started to drift off to sleep. I turned on my side and there was a hand that came around me and I could feel her body mold next to mine. I was fixing to say something, but sleep took me over.

Chapter 5(Sarah)

I awoke for a second and I had to realize where I was. Once I realized that I was still at Lavonna's, my heart stopped racing. I wondered what time it was because the room was still dark. The glow of the light from the fireplace danced along the walls and cast a small hint of light in the room. It was still comfortable; not hot. I was still sluggish from sleep. I just wanted to just lay down and sleep my worries away. At least in my sleep I didn't have to deal with reality. Even though my sleep was not peaceful, sometimes riddled with nightmares, I woke myself up screaming. Then I remembered Lavonna had slept in bed with me or was that a dream? I touched the other side of the bed and wondered if she had really slept with me and held me while brushing her fingers through my hair. I laughed and shrugged that thought from my head because it had to be a dream.

I slipped out of the bed and grabbed my phone on the nightstand. *Oh My God,* it was

1 o'clock in the afternoon. I hurried to the bathroom, my clothes were neatly folded with a toothbrush and other items to start my day.

My clothes smelled wonderful, and I was astonished to have been sleeping that hard not to know someone had been in here. I shrugged off the anxiety and started getting ready to leave.

As I was walking out on my way to the kitchen, calling Andy to come pick me up I ran straight into Lavonna. Of course, her steadying us both I dropped my phone.

"Are you ok and is this how we are always going to run into each other like this?"

With a playful grin on her face, I realized she was trying to make a joke. I just stared at her eyes and was caught in them like a drowning pull of a vampire's eyes.

Andy's voice startled me back to reality from behind Lavonna. Lavonna was back to her usual poker face that said everything and nothing at the same time.

"I am so sorry for sleeping so late."

"You needed the rest," she said.

Lavonna looked at Andy,

"Well, I will leave her in your capable hands" and walked off.

I stared as she walked away, she was captivating. Andy cleared his throat and giggled while handing me a cup of coffee just the way I liked it, and it smelled amazing.

"Let's go and sit and talk on the terrace; I will drive you back to your house after that to get some things."

I stopped following him and there was a flash of anger in my eyes as he turned around.

"What now?" Andy ran his hand through his hair which I knew he did when he was frustrated.

"Why would you drive me back to my house just to get some things. Where am I going?" I said confused.

"Back here of course till we can locate her." Andy replied.

"I am not running anymore Andy. I am tired, and this needs to stop. I love the life that I have built here, and it is time to face my past." I said with my face defiant.

"Yeah, a past that can get you killed. We have a meeting with Nelson at four this afternoon; so, you better be ready."

Nelson was the local Sheriff; he was very kind, honorable and towered over everyone. He had to be about 6'7. Nelson kept in shape which came from his military roots, and he ran a tight ship around town. I explained to Andy that I had been through the whole law thing. It was explained to me that until she tries to harm me or does something crazy, they can't do anything to her. But by then as always; it will be too late.

"I do not need you to fix my problems" I replied quickly.

I could feel my anger rising. I didn't want anything to happen to them or get them caught in something they didn't ask for.

"I love you like a sister, and I want my sister to stay with the living," Andy replied.

I sighed and knew I wasn't going to win this fight.

"Fine Andy, I'll agree only if I get to stay at my house because I am not going to keep staying here or your house. I have a house, and I refuse to let Jade take that away from me."

"I don't think that would be a good idea, Sarah" said Lavonna as she was walking up.

I turned and said "Why not? I am an adult, and I think I can make my own decisions."

"Really, why are you sitting there with your hands folded over your chest sulking like a child?" Lavonna replied with a chuckle.

My anger flared at Lavonna's statement. I got up, looked at Andy and told him, "I am ready please take me home."

He sat his cup on the table because I was already walking to the door.

"See you tonight Ms. Lively" I heard Lavonna say laughing.

I sat in Andy's jeep seething all the way to the police station.

Who the fuck does she think she is? No one tells me how to run my life.

I calmed down a little as we pulled into the police station. I had that eerie feeling that someone was watching me because all the hair stood up on the back of my neck. I started looking around, but everything looked like a normal beautiful day. I walked with Andy into the Sherriff's office wondering if this was going to be the biggest mistake that I have ever made.

Chapter 6(Sarah)

Nelson sat behind his desk in the cramped office which barely held two chairs and a desk, but he looked like he belonged there. I sat in the chair beside Andy, and I was more anxious now than I had been in a long time.

Memories of Jade's voice laced with threats of what she would do to me if I ever left or what she would do if police were to get involved. Even after leaving, her voice was still echoing in my ears. I could still hear her laughter as she reminded me that the police would never believe me. As I sit here now, I am worried about it and the fact that she was right. She made me look like I was the psycho, and she even went as far as putting a restraining order on me saying I tried to kill her. It had been 5 years, and my nightmares were still as vivid as the night I left her. She could con a con out of something, she was a smooth talker and could make anyone believe anything she said.

I lost everything and then she kept taking more; thinking I would come back or beg for her help.

Nelson was calling my name and when I felt a hand on my knee I jumped. Andy pulled back, and it was like coming out from under anesthesia. I looked at Andy and realized where I was. The tears just started flowing down my cheeks. I can't relive this again, I really thought I had covered my tracks this time. I should have known and not gotten myself into a false sense of security. Nelson slid the tissue box to me, and I took some and attempted to calm myself down. He genuinely looked concerned.

"Do you need anything else before we start?"

"I am ok." I replied breathing in and out trying to calm my nerves.

I started telling Sherriff Nelson everything all the way up to yesterday when she entered my house. Andy told Sherriff Nelson how they found me, and that Jade was standing over me when he and Lavonna walked in. Andy reached into his pocket and pulled out a piece of paper. The paper contained a notarized copy of Lavonna Black's statement. I was sitting there, and I knew I had to look like a buffoon because Andy said.

"Lavonna called a notary to the house when he had got there."

Sherriff Nelson's eyebrow raised for a moment, but he then went back to a blank cop face. He looked up at me.

"I am putting in a restraining order and a protection order. I will also for at least a couple of days have a deputy drive by your house and keep an eye on everything." He said with concern peaking through his blank cop face.

I let out my breath; I hadn't even realized I was holding it. I sat in that chair staring at Sherriff Nelson not believing what I was hearing. A second of doubt almost crept in because this was the first time that something was going in my favor. I shook my head and felt immediate strength.

I can get through this, and I am going to put a stop to you Jade. I thought to myself.

I rose from my seat and extended my hand to Sherriff Nelson to thank him.

He smiled and replied "Just doing my job. If you need anything call the station."

Andy and I walked out of the Sherriff station; the sun was blinding; I stopped and closed my eyes and let the sun beat down on my face. I felt a sense of relief like I haven't felt in years and confidence that everything was going to work out.

"Let's go get some coffee. I know the local coffee shop owner here in town and I hear the coffee is to die for and the one who owns it is not bad on the eyes either." Andy wiggled his eyebrows and laughed as we headed for the jeep.

"Well, I may skip it then because I ain't ready to be pushing up flowers yet" and we both laughed as we got into Andy's Jeep and headed to the Burnt Pelican.

Chapter 7(Sarah)

I stayed the day at the Burnt Pelican helping and just keeping myself busy. I felt better and safer than I had in years. I was thankful for Andy as well as Lavonna which my mind kept wandering back to. I was wondering what she would look like as my tongue was sliding down her …..

"Sarahhhhhh"

I jumped out of my thoughts with a wicked smirk on my face and started instantly blushing when I realized I was staring into Andy's eyes. He was smiling at me.

"Oh, you must tell me what you were thinking about. That had to be a juicy thought because your expression was almost sinful," he chuckled.

I could feel my cheeks grow even hotter.

"Nothing you would like to know."

I walked outside to sit on the patio and waited for Andy to come outside while I watched the sunset darken over the horizon.

I could do this, and no one was going to ever hurt me anymore. I breathed in the saltwater air and the wind blowing in my hair and closed my eyes to let go of the stress that was in my body. I opened my eyes as Andy was walking up with the best latte in the world.

Something about Andy's coffee made me feel safe and at home and I haven't had that feeling in years. Andy sat down and studied me for a minute.

"How are you feeling, Sarah…no lies either."

I contemplated how I felt and let the thought swirl in my mind. I looked at him.

"I believe for the first time in my life I can say I will be ok. I am thankful for you and Lavonna."

He raised an eyebrow; "Lavonnaaaaaa huhhh" as he drug out her name.

My cheeks are back to feeling like lava being poured onto my face.

"I knew it, you like her, don't you?" Andy screamed "I knew it. You know Lavonna has taken an interest in you as well" he said.

"I am a mess as you can see, and I am dealing with a lot." I rolled my eyes.

"She is a big girl Sarah she can take care of herself. I see the way y'all watch each other when y'all think no one is looking. I also see the way the two of you look at each other when you all think no one is watching. I can feel the tension between y'all vibrating." He leaned back looking out into the ocean.

I hummed and sat back in the chair and sipped on my latte. We watched as the sun set and basked in the cool breeze from the ocean. We were cleaning up the shop when Andy asked.

"Are you staying with me tonight?"

I thought about it.

"No thanks, I want my bed tonight."

He huffed but said "OK" and then ran his hands through his hair and asked,

"Are you sure?"

"Yes, I am sure everything will be ok." I replied leaning on the broom I was sweeping with.

"Ok then we are sleeping at your house" he said as he shrugged and walked off before I could even utter a word.

I exhaled boudly knowing that I wouldn't be able to change his mind, ok well, at least

I would have my own bed. *I sure wish I was* in *Lavonna's bed* I thought to myself, but I quickly shook that thought from my mind. Why am I so attracted to this woman and why is she in every one of my thoughts? I felt the tingling inside my thighs and the pulling of want and desire creeping up.

As we were pulling up to my house, I saw Lavonna's Range Rover. I looked at Andy, and he just shrugged.

"Did you set this up?" I asked.

"No, I didn't, she called and asked if I was staying with you tonight and that was it I promise."

We both got out of his jeep and Lavonna was leaning up against the door. My breath caught at the sight of her. The wind was blowing her hair, and the smell of coconut and honeysuckle reached out and ran through my nostrils. It was the smell that I took in last night as she eased in the bed with me and that is something I didn't tell Andy. I didn't need him having any more ammunition than he already had when it came to me and Lavonna. To be honest I felt safe in that bed with Lavonna, and I will always treasure that.

Chapter 8(Sarah)

I watched Lavonna closely as Andy and I walked up to my house. My eyes were hidden behind my dark shades because even now with the sun almost completely gone down the throbbing in my temples had made everything a little more sensitive. I let my eyes start from the top of her head to the bottom of her toes. As my gaze came back up, she had this smirk on her face like she knew what I was doing and liked the way I was doing it. Looking at her I could feel my face heat up. The smirk was gone and replaced with a dazzling smile. She pushed off the SUV and met us halfway. She spoke to Andy and then looked at me.

"Do you want to go pack a bag?" she questioned.

I must have looked as confused as I felt.

Lavonna responded, "you are staying at my house tonight."

I had recovered from the look of utter confusion, and it was replaced with anger.

"I most certainly am not. I have my own house; I don't need to go anywhere, and I am not getting told what the fuck to do tonight."

I walked toward the door to unlock it with Lavonna and Andy trailing me. They were bickering back and forth, I opened the door and stopped so abruptly Lavonna ran straight into me. I turned with anger in my face.

"You can see your way out."

 I then turned to Andy "You can go home too."

He put up his hands and said, "are you sure?"

"Yes, and if I need you, I will call."

"OK I will check on you a little later" he replied and then he turned around and left.

I walked into the house and laid everything on the kitchen island. I turned around and looked at Lavonna.

"I am still wondering why you're here, Ms. Black," with my arms crossed around my chest.

I was seething with anger. She had this look on her face, and all I could use to describe it was 'dominance'. She took a step forward and I stood my ground with my anger taking root. My anger was like roots in the floorboard and I wasn't going to give an inch. She took another step closer to me, she had her hands in her pockets, and she stopped. I was still rooted but a little shaky as she took another step forward and before I realized it, I hit the wall behind me. *Well damn so much for me standing my ground.* She was so close to me, my heart was in my throat, her scent was intoxicating, she put both her hands, one on each side of my face on the wall and leaned into me. Our faces were so close. Her nose almost touching mine.

She whispered, "now why would I leave and be worried about you all night."

My throat was dry, and I tried to hold onto my anger, but all my mind and body could think about was how soft her lips would be if I kissed them. *Why am I thinking about this right now?* My body was betraying me, I could feel myself getting wet.

I am a submissive in the BDSM world and this right here is a fantasy come true. She was still so close that I could feel her breath. She had me pinned against the wall. I finally collected my thoughts and said looking into her eyes.

"I am a grown woman, and I don't need you for anything. I will be fine by myself."

I smiled on the inside because my voice didn't crack once. My legs felt like they were going to give out.

She smiled and leaned in closer to me and whispered in my ear, "I am fully aware that you are a full-grown woman, and I don't like you telling me no kitten. So, pack you a bag or I will do it for you. You are coming to my house tonight one way or the other because no is not in my vocabulary and trust me it won't be in yours for long."

She leaned away from me and walked into the living room. I was left there against the wall trying to relearn how to breathe as I groaned to myself. I knew I was not going to get anywhere arguing. So, what did I do? I went and packed an overnight bag like the good girl I am and the good girl I want to be.

Chapter 9(Sarah)

I was sitting on the passenger side of Lavonna's Range Rover sulking and thinking *how the hell did I let her talk me into this*. The ride was a quiet ride, but it was a peaceful silence. I laid back and let the seat warmers do their thing. Even if it is hot outside sometimes the heat helps relieve some tension.

I must have been more comfortable than I thought because the next thing I knew Lavonna's hand was on my shoulder slightly shaking me and saying my name in that low sultry voice of hers. I came to quickly.

"We have made it home" she whispered.

Home, I immediately thought what it would be like to live in a home like this. Humph, well I guess we can all dream right. I got out slowly feeling the stress from the day. I shrugged it off and went to the back to get the suitcase that was packed in a rush. We both reached for the handle at the same time. The shock when our hands touched was like playing with electricity.

"Go ahead and go in and I will get your bags."

I argued for a minute but then she gave me that look; I shut my mouth. What was this woman doing to me I was not her submissive. She had not earned or wanted my submissiveness. So, *why the hell did I just do what she said?* It wasn't out of fear, more out of lust. I scolded myself because it had been over two years since I had let off some steam in a scene.

Lord knows my ex-Jade didn't dabble in that world. She called me disgusting and made me feel bad about myself for liking those things and of course I wasn't allowed to touch her either. For a lesbian woman, the worst thing ever is not being able to touch and please your partner.

"Ms. Lively, are you coming or are you staying outside the whole night?" Lavonna asked standing in the doorway.

I had gotten lost in my thoughts and was completely embarrassed. I shook my head and followed Lavonna into the house. As we walked in, we passed the bedroom I had slept in last night.

"Am I not sleeping in the same bedroom as last night?" I asked confused.

"No, you will be sleeping in mine" she responded.

I stopped in my tracks. "Who the fuck do you think you are?"

She stopped and set my suitcase down and turned to me. She stepped toward me, and I was riddled with anger, this seemed to be a thing and dammit I was holding onto this anger as I looked at her.

"I am thankful for everything you have done Ms. Black, but I am fucking leaving because you have lost your fucking mind to think you can order me around like you fucking own me. That's not happening."

I was walking away, damn the clothes and everything.

"I will get Andy to retrieve my things."

I pulled out my phone to call Andy. I told Andy that if he didn't come to get me, I would call an Uber. She grabbed my hand and spun me around to meet her gaze. The need in her eyes was almost palpable and my breath caught in my chest. My lungs couldn't get enough air and then the look was gone.

"We are trying to protect you, Sarah. You have been hurt so much you don't know when to trust or even if you can trust anymore. Stay here tonight and if you want to leave tomorrow you can but let someone take care of you for a change. Let someone show you how to be cared for. You are so infuriating!"

She still had a hold of my wrist, and she sighed and mumbled "if you were mine, I would be punishing you right now."

I knew what she meant by punishing me. *Is she really a Domme* I thought? I said, "OK but only for the night."

She looked at me and smiled as she let go of my wrist. She turned and as she grabbed my bag and walked to the bedroom, she said "good girl."

Chapter 10(Sarah)

I walked into her bedroom, and it was huge. It was like walking into a fairytale, a very dark fairytale. She was standing by the end of the bed, and she placed my suitcase on the lounge chair.

"So weird question."

She stopped and looked at me and said, "OK what is it?"

"Are you a Villain or a hero?" I asked.

"Well, that is an off the wall question." She stood silent for a minute and shrugged "I would take the Villain part."

She walked over to a gorgeous wood sliding door. I figured it was the bathroom door. The more I looked at the door the more I found myself walking towards it. It was made from dark mahogany wood but the details in it were gorgeous. I was so transfixed on the door I did not realize that Lavonna had walked up behind me. She leaned in and I felt her breath graze my ear which made everything inside tingle and everything outside shiver.

"Do you like it," she whispered.

The door had a carving of a woman on her knees naked. Her hands were bound behind her back and the ropes intertwined her body. Her hair was braided, and it was slung over her shoulders. Then it hit me it was Shabari a form of rope bonding.

Still staring at the door, I told Lavonna.

"This is beyond gorgeous, and the technique of Shabari is gorgeous."

She raised an eyebrow and looked pleased with herself.

"I had it commissioned from a local carpenter. Sarah, you should have seen the look on his face when I explained what I wanted on the door, it was priceless." She walked through the door, and I heard water starting to run.

"How hot do you like your baths?"

I leaned around the door, and I was awestruck again at the sight of the bathroom but shook myself out of it.

"I don't need……"

She stopped me before I could even finish the sentence and said "no sweetness that is not what we agreed on when you said that you would spend the night. So how hot do you take your baths?"

"I like them hot but not so hot that it raises the temperature too much to enjoy it." I replied looking around the bathroom.

"Um hum" she said feeling the water.

I watched her as she sat on the side and ran her hand under the water to check the temperature.

"Are you allergic or sensitive to anything?" she asked.

"No, I am not at least that I know of anyway."

She started putting things in the water. While she was doing that, I walked around the bathroom just taking everything in. The huge, jetted tub in the middle of the floor was big enough to hold two people: maybe more. The marble was floor to ceiling. The gold and black complimented each other. I am not too much for gold but the way the marble was made it looked so elegant. If you ever watched anime, this bathroom resembled the ones in an anime film because it has a shower and tub just in one spacious room. Off to the right the shower spanned the entire wall and on one side a bench if you wanted to sit down. The showerheads made me so jealous. I was walking around spotting things on the walls. If you didn't know what you were looking for or was not in the BDSM lifestyle you would overlook them.

I walked closer to where the bench was, and I ran my hand over the marble. It felt like a covering. My hand was on the wall, Lavonna walked up behind me and put her hand over mine. We pushed, the marble disappeared and there was a hardpoint there.

"I knew it," I squeaked.

I started looking around the room and could see square places everywhere.

I turned to her and asked, "do you have hardpoints all around this bathroom?"

Lavonna just looked at me and said, "you are the first person to ever notice them."

I blushed and said "sorry."

She laughed; it was like rubbing velvet on my skin.

"What do you have to be sorry about? I am fucking impressed even my submissive's have missed them." She looked very pleased.

"The women that you were having dinner with, were you vetting them? I am sorry that is none of my business." I quickly said.

She tilted my head up so my eyes met hers.

"You have nothing to be sorry about kitten because I am, open with who I am. A lot of people cannot take the matter of fact, not time for bullshit me. Now let's get you in the bath. I am going to change. I will knock when I get back to see if you are still in the bath and I will come and wash your hair."

I nodded because I have never had this type of treatment, it was always something that I craved but never had. I had the usual aftercare from scenes at the dungeons I had visited from time to time, but this was on another level. I was left staring at her after she slid the door shut.

Tonight, you are going to let go. If you regret it tomorrow that will be tomorrow to deal with but not tonight. I told myself.

I sank down in the bath and I could smell roses and coconut. I inhaled the scent and just leaned back and let the hot water pull the stress out of my body. I had my eyes closed when I heard a soft knock on the door. I knew I was naked, but I felt at home and comfortable, and all the bubbles hid every inch of my body. There was a mirror at the end of the room that ran along the whole back wall. I inhaled and said "come in" before I lost the nerve.

I watched as Lavonna came in wearing a pair of basketball shorts and a muscle tank top. She had taken her bra off and her nipples were hard. I didn't even realize that I was clenching my thighs together in the water. I watched as she came closer in the mirror and walked to the corner. There she picked up a small wooden bench and set it at the edge of the tub. I could see her reflection in the mirror as she leaned down and whispered in my ear "Just relax kitten."

I closed my eyes and sank into the water as she started to wash my hair. I heard her rumbling through the drawers getting things out but tonight I was going to put my trust in someone, and I'll deal with the consequences tomorrow. She sit down on the bench, lathering and running her fingers through my hair. Massaging my scalp from the back to the top and boy did it feel good. She washed the shampoo out and started putting in the conditioner.

"I want to wait 5 minutes before washing the conditioner out so lean back for me."

Her hands slid into the water and started massaging my shoulders as she worked her way up my neck. I was fit to be tied because with every touch I wanted her so much more.

"Can I ask you something Lavonna?"

"Ask away," she said.

"Those women that you were having dinner with I know you were vetting them but were you going over subcontracts with them?"

"Yes, I was," she replied.

"Do you have a sub now?" I asked.

"No, I have been in the market for a few months." She replied still massaging my shoulders.

"So, I'm going out on a limb here. If I were to ask you if we could do a scene, would you be willing to do it with no strings attached?"

There was silence for a second and she replied, "normally I have no interaction without a contract. I also don't enter into scenes with a non-disclosure agreement and being tested for STD's."

"OK I was just wondering. I completely understand. I cannot hold a candle to those women anyway; I look nothing like them."

She told me to open my eyes and look at her, so I looked through the mirror and she was looking straight into me like she was staring into my soul.

"You are gorgeous, you must know that. Also, I have been watching you and you check off every box that I look for in a sub. When's the last time that you had a scene" she asked.

"Hmm, let me think about it. It has probably been at least two years since I had a scene and two years since I've been to dungeons. When I moved to this town I stopped going to the dungeons. Jade, the one that is stalking me now always told me I was disgusting for wanting the extra stuff in the bedroom. She made me feel like it was wrong, and I was sick for wanting it. So, I had to relearn that it's OK for what I crave in the bedroom. Because things that I desire run a little dark."

"I like dark" she replied. "So, tell me a little bit about your kinks. A Reader's Digest version will do for tonight. What are your hard limits, things that you allow, and your safe word?" she asked.

"Well, the reader's digest version is I love Shabari/bondage. I love sensation play and my senses taken away. I can do penetration if it is body safe silicone. I'm OK with light impact play but it has been a long time since I've had that. Those are a few things that I'm into. My hard limits are no anal and I already have my nipple rings. I am not a pain slut, but I do enjoy a little pain with pleasure. My safe word is dragonfly."

"That's an interesting safe word" she replied.

She was washing the conditioner out and slowly massaging a light rose oil into my hair. The soft scent of roses filled the room, and I inhaled the scent as her fingers caressed their way through my hair.

"Ok Ms. Lively let's do a scene but a very minimal scene and then tomorrow we will forget this ever happened or we can go over some contracts if you are interested."

She slowly combed through my wet hair.

"Let me go prepare and I want you to relax and take all the time you need and everything in the bathroom you can use. So, make yourself comfortable. When you are ready, come into the room naked and lay down on the bed." She replied as she was drying her hands off on a towel.

Chapter 11(Sarah)

As I lay in the water feeling relaxed as ever with a Cheshire cat grin on my face, it hit me. I slipped coming up from the water. I found myself splashing and spurting.

Wondering what had I asked for and what was I doing? I was trying to breathe; it was like all the air had seeped out of the room and my vision grew dark. I knew I had to calm myself before I drowned myself by passing out. What a way to go, excited and passed away from drowning after a panic attack. That cleared my head a little and I stared at my reflection in the mirror.

I scolded myself and got out of the tub transfixed on the mirror walking toward it and leaving watery footprints behind me on the marble floor. I let my gaze flow down my body admiring every curve and every scar. I was beautifully scarred, but I made it out alive so fuck yes, I am proud of myself. I let my hand follow the curves and the outlines of the scars that were on my body. You deserve this in every way so get out of your head. I walked over to the tub and let the water out. I picked up the rose oil that Lavonna had left on the side of the tub. The rose oil softened my skin and gave me the scent of freshly cut roses in bloom. With my skin still soft and smelling of roses, I headed from the bathroom into the bedroom.

As I entered the bedroom I walked over to the fireplace. I stood there as the flames from the fireplace danced on my skin. I turned and was frozen in my tracks as I saw Lavonna sitting in the leather chair that she turned toward the bathroom door. She was sitting there holding her drink in one hand and letting her eyes roam from the top of my head to my feet and then back up. There was a wildness in her eyes a hunger that burned and just that look had my pussy jumping. I knew at that moment I would never forget this night.

Lavonna got up and set her drink on the coffee table. She walked over to me and before I realized what I was doing my back was against the wall and a small yelp had slipped from my mouth. She looked like a lion stalking her prey and without warning she had caught me. Suddenly her hand was around my throat holding me against the wall. Her breath tickling my ear from being so close.

"Are you sure you want all of this My little Snake-Doctor." She whispered.

My mind was everywhere, my heart was racing, and I was trying to make sense of what she said as my body was turning on me. I could feel the wetness starting to run down my thighs. Her hand loosened from my throat.

"Why did you call me your snake-doctor?"

She laughed and closed her hand around my throat again. I could feel my heart racing. Her lips grazed my ear as she spoke softly into it.

"Let me tell you why," with her other hand gliding down my curves.

My chest heaved up and down as she traced my body to her satisfaction.

"Calm down my sweetness. I want you to hear every word I say, and I want to feel how bad you want me."

Her hand found my breast and kneading then slightly pinching my nipple. I couldn't tell what I needed more, air or her. She loosened her grip for me to draw breath and as I was fixing to speak, she placed a finger on my mouth.

"Shhhh," she spoke into my ear "I haven't even started telling you why yet. I am going to let go of your throat and you are going to be a good girl and not speak."

She was so close staring into my eyes "nod if you understand me."

I nodded as best as I could with her hand around my throat. She kept her eyes on me and slowly let go of my throat. I stood there staring into her eyes.

"Do not take your eyes off me." she commanded.

With her hands she found my breast again. She started kneading my nipples between her fingers and slowly working her way down my body over my hips all while she stared into my eyes.

"Open your legs sweetness."

I opened them without saying a word, wanting to be the good girl she asked me to be. One hand on the wall beside me while the other traced all my curves and slowly glided up my thighs. I could feel the moan about to escape my lips when I heard,

"Ah ah not a sound remember."

It took real strength to swallow that moan.

"Oh, sweetness I haven't even made it to that sweet pussy, and you are dripping wet; fuck me," she growled.

She grabbed me by the hand and led me to the bed. I could see the ropes and cuffs hanging. They were not there earlier. Blood red ropes with black cuffs at the end.

"Lay down" she commanded.

I climbed on the bed. As she placed the blind fold on me, she asked me to tell her my safe word again. I licked my lips and said "Dragonfly."

She leaned down and brushed her lips over my ear and said, "so here is the reason why you are my Snake-Doctor."

 She kissed my neck before I heard her rustling with the restraints.

 "Let me tell you a folklore about Dragonflies. Listen well sweetness as I get you ready for what I can give you."

She started placing my hands in the restraints.

"Dragonflies are known as snake doctors. They follow snakes around and stitch up injuries that the snake sustains especially when the snake is left in pieces."

I felt the last restraint close tightly around my foot. I felt Lavonna straddle me and then her hand was at my throat again.

She whispered in my ear "you are the snake doctor, and I am the snake, so it is a fitting name for you. Now let me show you why no one will ever be a right fit for you but me. After tonight you will only crave me."

She then bit and slowly ran her tongue up my ear. She got off the bed and without warning all the restraints were pulled. This made my legs open wide and pulled my arms away from my body. I felt the warm breeze touch my center. A chill ran up my body and made me shiver. Feathers tease my nipples and work their way down my body. The sensation was overwhelming. The light tickle against my skin gave me goosebumps and made my skin hot to the touch. I groaned as Lavonna's hands slowly worked their way down my body and up my thighs.

"Fuck sweetness I can't get over how wet you are," she whispered.

Her hand hovered over my clit as I tried to roll my hips to push her hand to my center.

"Na sweetness not just yet," Lavonna whispered.

I let out a soft whimper. I felt the coolness and the sting of the ice before it touched me. There was also a subtle softness of something else, I focused on the path it was traveling trying to decipher it. Then it hit me, she had ice in her mouth and that was the subtle softness of her lips tracing my body.

She breathed out, "good girl now lay back and enjoy."

Lavonna rubbed the ice across my nipples which brought them to a peak. The sensation between her mouth and the ice was more than I could bear. She glided the ice up my neck, next to my lips and let it sit there between us melting and running down my body. Once it melted, she used her tongue to open my mouth as she kissed me slowly and passionately. The kiss grew deep and ravenous. I moaned into her mouth as her hand went between my folds.

She growled into my mouth "so fucking wet."

She slipped one finger in me; I gasped and slowly rose for air. Then she slipped another finger in me and then another working them in and out of me slowly.

"Oh my god kitten you are so fucking tight."

I wanted more, I wanted her, and I wanted everything she could give me. Her thumb was massaging my clit. I felt the rush and I knew I was close. Lavonna started working her hands faster and just as I was about to fall over the edge she pulled back. I lay there whimpering and breathless.

"Not yet sweetness, when I make you cum it will be on my tongue. I want to see if you are as sweet as you smell."

Trailing kisses all the way down my body. She was between my legs and feeling the warm air as she blew on my folds.

"You smell amazing sweetness. Let's see what you taste like."

Her mouth descended onto my clit. She began sucking and rolling it so slowly around in her mouth. She continued sucking and giving me extra pressure, speeding up bringing me to that peak only to pull back. I wanted her so bad, I wanted to let go of all the stress I was holding on to.

Lavonna breathed out as if she could read my mind, "Sweetness let go."

Then she claimed my clit and I was suddenly tipping over the edge. I let go, I screamed and pulled on the restraints as I let the orgasm wash over me riding wave after wave of ecstasy. Lavonna's lips touched mine and I tasted me. I kissed her with my taste between us.

She drew back and said, "sweetness I am not done yet you needed a release of sensation but now I am going to fuck you."

She was suddenly between my legs. I felt the strap she was wearing touch my thighs as she positioned herself.

"Tonight, you are mine and mine alone. I want to hear my name on your lips."

She slid into me with one smooth motion.

"Fuck…. I knew you were ready for me."

Lavonna placed her hand around my throat while she thrusted in and out harder and harder. As she tightened her hand around my throat again, she asked,

"Whose are you?"

She loosened her hand.

"I am yours."

"I want you to say it again my little snake doctor, whose are you?"

She kneaded my breast pinching my nipples while fucking me harder and harder. I felt the pressure building.

"I want you to cum for me sweetness" and she increased her pace.

I was falling over the edge and that is when her teeth clamped onto my breast as she brought me to ecstasy again. I screamed out and felt the orgasm run up my body and, in that moment, I was free of everything, no worries and no stress. Tears started falling down the sides of my eyes. I rode the pleasure as long as I could.

Lavonna took the blindfold off. She started unfastening the restraints and when all were unfastened, she soothed me as she whispered,

"I will be right back lay right here."

I mumbled "ok" feeling sated and a little sleepy. I heard the faint sound of water running in the background and as I felt her slide behind me, she turned me over on my back and told me to spread my legs. The towel was warm and as she cleaned me up, I groggily asked what I could do for her. Lavonna smiled that animalistic grin and said,

"There will be time for that but tonight was a taste for you and a moment to let go of some of that stress."

She slipped in behind me and pulled me close.

"Sweetness sleep tonight."

As I was falling asleep, I thought I heard her say *I have gotten a taste of you and now there will be no way of letting you go.* I drifted off with her rubbing her hands through my hair.

Chapter 12(Sarah)

I woke in a dark room and had to realize where I was as this was the second day this had happened. I reached out my hand and felt for Lavonna, but her side was empty. I felt a slight soreness in between my legs, and everything came rushing back to me. I placed my fingers on my lips where she had kissed me and smiled. I felt better and I could breathe even though it wasn't a huge scene, it had taken the edge off. It was what I needed and desired.

I lay there deciding and knew I had to put a stop to Jade. It was like I was renewed and wanted to take my life back. I slipped out of bed and slowly walked to the bathroom. It had been a while since I have had things that rough, but it brought a smile to my face. I walked over to the shower and turned it on.

I went to the mirror and stared into it. I stared at where Lavonna had bitten me and there was a set of perfect teeth marks on my breast. Rubbing my hand over them gently.

I got in the shower and there was a little discomfort over the bite marks and still a little soreness in between my thighs but I felt like a weight was lifted and I could breathe. I let the water rush over my skin. I dried off and put the rose oil over my skin.

I must get me some of this, I said to myself.

After drying my hair, I put on a small amount of makeup and finished with a black and red sundress that hugged me in all the right places. It barely covered the bite mark but if I don't go running, I figured everything would stay in place. I walked out of the room and was walking to the kitchen when I overheard Lavonna in her study. Stopping and trying to figure out do I say something or do I just head to the kitchen.

I was starving. I usually am after a scene. I decided to see if she wants me to cook us up something. I walked over to the door that was slightly ajar when I heard Lavonna speak my name, but it was in conjunction with whoever she was speaking on the phone with. I stilled and felt so much fear. So many thoughts ran through my head, and I could tell Lavonna was angry by the tone she was using. I could barely make it out when I leaned on the door and forgot it was ajar and I fell into the room.

Lavonna turned and the look on her face was rage as she looked down at me and then, like I had imagined, she replaced it with her sultry look. She placed the phone on the receiver without a word and walked over to me as I was still on the floor pushing myself to get up. She reached out her hand and helped me off the floor.

"Well Ms. Lively that was certainly an entrance." She chuckled as I slowly pulled my hand from hers.

"Is everything ok" and nodded towards the phone.

She waved it off. "Yes, just dealing with a business matter don't worry yourself" and turned her attention back to me.

The smile she gave me would have melted glaciers.

"How are you feeling Ms. Lively?" Lavonna asked, "I do hope you got some good, needed rest and are feeling better this morning."

I smiled sheepily and responded "yes, a little sore but that is to be expected due to everything that took place last night. I was coming to see if you wanted breakfast, I was going to whip up something."

Lavonna said, "Luna can make us anything that we want."

I waved her off.

"Let Luna sit this one out; I'll do the cooking."

Lavonna's eyebrow raised and she smirked and said, "OK well Ms. Lively, I look forward to the meal."

She walked out and started towards the kitchen. I fell in step behind her, but my mind was going ninety to nothing about the business matter and I knew I heard my name in the mix.

What did I have to do with any business of Lavonna Blacks?

Lavonna stopped and turned around. I had not realized it and I ran straight into her. She wrapped her arms around me before I could get out, I'm sorry.

"Sweetness I could get used to this."

My mind was telling me to run while my heart was telling me another thing. Even though I knew Lavonna could be dangerous I had sunk into her embrace. I smelled the honeysuckle again and I whispered.

"Honeysuckle by day and coconut by night."

Like she was two different people. Lavonna started laughing.

"Sarah, you surprise me yet again no one can ever figure out the honeysuckle."

I breathed her in and exhaled.

"Well growing up in the country our back fence was overrun by honeysuckle. You had to pull the stem to bring that one bead of sweet juice out; it was great."

The smell of honeysuckle she gave off was so soft and not overwhelming. I smiled up at Lavonna, "you remind me of home."

Lavonna squeezed me tight and whispered in my ear "I can be your home if you let me."

My throat was suddenly dry, I let go and stepped out of Lavonna's embrace "well this is not getting breakfast cooked" and I went into the kitchen.

I was getting used to where everything was in the kitchen and moving about it like I had a purpose. Lavonna was leaning against the wall and just watching me with a smile. She watched me while I cooked. When I looked at her there was a flash of desire in her eyes, but it was there for a split second and then gone. She pushed off the wall after I pulled the bacon out of the oven and started walking toward me. Electricity ran up my body.

"Ms. Lively, you look right at home in my kitchen."

I was holding a metal mixing bowl for the waffles I was going to make and the closer she got to me the more I wanted to run.

"Run I dare you…..kitten I will catch you and when I do, I will take you right then and there."

I stood still as she walked and was then right in front of me.

"Good little prey stay right where you are."

My back was to the black marbled island that sat in the middle of the kitchen, it was cool to the touch. She stared into my eyes as she took the bowl and sat it down with a clang on the island. My instincts kicking in and I started to run. I was almost at the door when her hand caught my wrist and pushed me back to the island. Placing both of her hands on each side of me and growled low in my ear. "I caught you. Now let's see how wet you are," one hand went to my thighs, and slowly glided it up as she growled into my ear "spread those pretty legs for me."

My body reacted as I did what I was told. She reached my lips rubbing them,

"Oooo…..no panties Ms. Lively such a bad girl and you are dripping wet already. Are you always this wet?"

I had my eyes closed and wanted her right here and now, fuckkkk. Knowing someone could walk in at any moment made me even wetter. She ran her hands down my arms and then placed them around my hips. "Hold on kitten" and before I knew it, she picked me up and placed me on the counter. I let out a yelp. Her hand back at my entrance "look at me" she commanded and as our eyes met, pushing her fingers inside me, and I gasped and closed my eyes and Lavonna growled her voice filled with desire.

"No kitten keep your eyes on me."

I stared into her eyes, seeing into her soul, and falling more into her glare. Pushing her third finger in me sliding in and out making sure I felt every thrust. It felt like eternity. I felt my skin grow hot to the touch. Desire and need ran through me, and I was going to give it to her. I met every thrust pushing her fingers inside me deeper. As she kissed me it was animalistic, like she was ravenous and could not get sated. Working her kisses down and I felt her pull her fingers out of me and she brought them to my mouth.

"Open your mouth and taste your sweet juices I want you to suck my fingers clean."

My lips wrapped around her fingers sucking my juices from them. When I had sucked every bit of me off her fingers she smiled and said,

"Good girl and good girls get good rewards, are you ready kitten?"

Her face was suddenly between my legs, spreading my legs and my hands trying to keep me upright. She breathed on my clit and the sensation drove me wild. Then I felt her mouth on my clit slowly working it and I felt my orgasm building. Damn, I was right there.

 She pulled back a little, "not yet kitten you taste so good I don't want you to cum just yet."

I whimpered and I begged. She started slowly licking up all my juices. She was sucking at my clit plunging her tongue in and out, knowing when to slow down. I finally could not bear it anymore and I rocked my hips toward her wanting more. She obliged and quickened her pace, matching my hip thrusts. I felt the orgasm building and I put my hands in Lavonna's hair and pushed her face into me more. I fell over the edge screaming her name.

I was adjusting myself when Andy came walking through the door.

Lavonna with that smirk on her face and leaned into me and whispered, "I wonder how well you will handle all that wetness with no panties, huh love?"

She walked away laughing as Andy looked up from his phone and said, "did I miss something or is it something that I should be missing," wagging his eyebrows.

I shoved him and told him to help me finish cooking so we could bring the food out to the table.

Chapter 13(Sarah)

I had gotten a call earlier that day that someone wanted a last-minute in-home cook for an Anniversary. Lavonna was not happy, but I told her I was not going to let my business suffer for Jade, so we came to a compromise. I would come back to her house after finishing for the night.

Andy dropped me off at my house. He looked worried but I reassured him that I would be fine. It seemed like I had been gone for so long, but it had only been a couple of days. Andy asked again if I was sure I was going to be ok and I waved him off. I waited for him to leave, and I let go of the breath that I was holding. *I got this* I said aloud to build my confidence up.

Andy checked each and every room before he left. I told myself I wasn't going to let Jade win. I relaxed and walked out on the balcony and breathed in the ocean air. I could almost taste the saltiness on my tongue. I let all my worries drain out of me as I breathed out. I wanted to pack a few things that were mine and some clothes that I would want to have at Lavonna's. I was rummaging through my drawer and realizing I did not have anything even close to sexy to wear. Ugh I scolded myself knowing I should have always had a what if outfit. I threw in my pj's and went to get what I needed from the bathroom.

I glanced up in the mirror and noticed that my reflection was smiling ear to ear. I got my things ready for the night and headed to do my errands. I stopped by the butchers and farmer's market. I was so looking forward to tonight. I love love!!

I put the address and sang along to the radio. The drive was beautiful. Palm trees turning to pine trees and the leaves starting to change color from green to oranges to browns they flowed so well. I was grinning ear to ear; nothing could take this happiness away. It began to feel like I was driving forever, and it was becoming increasingly isolated. They did tell me they rented out this gorgeous house on one of the nearby lakes. This was going to be great.

I finally turned into a winding road. The house was beautiful, it was a two-story log cabin. They told me the code to get in and start setting everything up. I still had five hours till they made it here, but I wanted everything to be magnificent. I brought in the bags and after a few trips back and forth I had everything in. I set two alarms, one for forty-five minutes before they would get there and then ten minutes to get all the candles lit. This also allowed me some time to throw on something to meet them and leave them to their meal.

I placed my ear buds in and started working away at cutting the potatoes. Music blaring in my ears I laid the knife down and was fixing to get a pot of hot water on to boil when a hand appeared startling me. As the hand covered my nose and mouth with a rag, I grabbed at the knife but while grabbing for it my world started to go dark. I pushed through and picked up the knife and slashed the hand that was covering my nose and mouth. I heard Jade curse, but my world had already started to fade to black in that moment.

I woke up with a start and the headache was instant. Feeling dizzy and on the verge of throwing up with a total cotton mouth. I slowly started opening my eyes again trying to get my eyes to adjust. I tried to move and realized my arms and legs were bound. My pulse started picking up and my heart was beating out of my chest. I noticed I was in my pjs that I had packed for Lavonna's. I pulled at my restraints and the more I pulled the tighter they were becoming.

Then I heard her laughter, and it made my body run cold like I was encased in ice. It slowly came back to me. Before I blacked out hearing Jade curse when I slashed her hand with the knife.

"Oh, you got me pretty good princess," Jade said as she was holding up her hand.

There was blood that had trailed down her arm.

"Probably going to need stitches."

Jade walked up to the bed, her finger trailing up my body leaving goosebumps in their wake; it was not the good kind. She stared at me.

"I finally found you, I always told you that you could never leave me."

"Are you fucking delusional," I spat at her? I fucking left your ass and ran across the world to get away from you; no one wants you."

She slapped me and then leaned into me putting her fingers on each side of my jaw and pressed the pressure points.

Tears sliding down the sides of my face she leaned in and said

"That's better sweetheart, are you not happy with what I had to learn for you? I learned these knots especially for you. I thought you liked pain. Hummm, your disgusting fetishes and I learned all of this for you" she screamed in my face, "and you aren't appreciative. You never see what I do for you, you are so fucking selfish."

Jade's fingers were pressing down so hard I knew I was going to have bruises on each side of my face. Well, it wouldn't be the first time. Jade would always do that when I talked back because it was always a way to bring me to my knees. The pain of this technique was so instant and intense. Scared this time she was going to end up dislocating my jaw.

Her eyes were wild, *why did I not see this in her before?* I cursed myself for letting my emotions get the best of me. I started counting in my head to calm me. Jade let go of my face and sat on the bed.

"I came to get you back but now I don't know what to do with you since I saw you with that other woman. I am disgusted with you. How could you do that to me? You fucking cheated on me," Jade yelled in my face.

She was crazed and unstable, my mouth was hurting so bad. I stayed quiet and didn't say anything because I didn't know what was going to happen if I provoked her. She got up and started pacing the floor back and forth. I slowly started taking in the surroundings trying to slow my mind and figure out what to do next. I looked around this room and noticed that it didn't have any windows from what I could see. The bed was a king sized four postered bed. She had me tied to each poster. I was spread and the ropes were cutting into my legs and wrist. I knew not to struggle because this was a knot that if you struggled it got tighter.

I lay very still while Jade was still pacing a hole in the floor. I looked around again and noticed the plush carpets. The room was huge and there were French doors that led into the master suite. There was one door that led out of the room. If I was in any other circumstance this room would be amazing. The carpet was plush and red, I could cocoon myself in front of the wall high fireplace in the corner of the room.

I wondered to myself *if this is the end and will I be able to make it out alive this time.*

Tears started welling up in my eyes, making my vision blurry. I turned my head away from Jade to let them roll down my face. I knew that no one would be coming to save me. Why would they? I had no family. I isolated myself and I knew Andy would look for me but to be honest I didn't hold any hope. Lavonna wouldn't care either, I was probably just a lay to her. She wouldn't involve herself in this mess, would she? I felt myself losing hope as tears continuously flowed down my face.

Chapter 14 (Lavonna)

I turned around and faced my head of security Leon and the look on my face had to be terrifying because Leon cast his eyes downward. Leon had been with me for years and had seen some of my rougher moments and he knew this rage.

"You fucking lost her."

I let the words slowly come out in a growl. Trying to control my anger, I knew Leon and if Jade had bested Leon, she was good. This meant that I could not take her lightly. He knew it was past apologies at this point, so he stood there waiting for me.

"What is the plan of action?" I asked pacing the floors.

"I have our best guys out there looking and trying to locate some sort of trail or anything that would shed light on Ms. Lively's whereabouts." Leon replied.

I gazed back at my bookcase where the snake bookends were. Leon walked into my line of vision as my anger was there again like a flashing wave of lava burning me from the inside out.

"Lavonna it is not worth it," Leon pleaded. He said, "You told me that was over, and we weren't going to back to that lifestyle."

Sarah was right, I had a past and that past was very dark, a past full of secrets. Leon and Andy were the only ones that knew.

Why is Sarah affecting me this much?

I knew I wanted a new sub in the bedroom but since I looked into Sarah's emerald eyes and the way they change colors with whatever mood she is in, I have been lost in her. I needed to have her and call her mine and now someone has taken that from me. She must have not opened the envelope that I had sent home with her either because I had sent her a sub contract.

I looked up into Leon's cold gaze.

"You have until tonight to find Sarah, if not all bets are off. But either way I want Jade captured because this ends now. Get me all the information you have on Jade Sharp, and I want everything you have on how Sarah was taken."

I am so glad I asked questions when Sarah was telling me about Jade. Jade did not know she had royally fucked up this time, but this time will be her last. Leon walked out without another word, and I sank into my desk chair staring at the Snake Bookend that reminded me every day of where I had come from. I snapped out of my thoughts when Andy busted into the room.

"Where is she Lavonna I can't get a hold of Sarah, and I came straight here."

I had never seen him so distraught. Sarah had come into our lives and took hold. She was never going to let go and I didn't want her to. Trying to calm Andy was like telling a tornado to stop. I poured him a drink and told him to sit down. As he took the glass and his seat I went and sat behind the desk. He started to take a drink but placed it on the desk. He gripped the glass so tight I thought he was going to break it.

"It is my fault" as he ran his hands through his hair. "I knew I shouldn't have let her go alone but she insisted; the fucking stubborn woman she is. I thought you had security on her Lavonna what fucking happened?"

He looked at me wildly with anger. My anger was rising but I snuffed it out knowing it wasn't his fault and he had a right to be angry. I calmly looked at him.

"Jade lost them, she is not an ordinary person. Andy, she was able to lose Leon." I replied.

He had a look of shock and then just sat there for a moment.

"Shit Jade is fucking dangerous Lavonna."

"I know, I am getting all the information on her, and they are out looking for Sarah now we will find her."

"But what if" he trailed off.

"I won't let that happen Andy. She is mine and no one takes what is mine, you know that."

I got up and walked to the bookshelf where the black mamba with ruby eyes bookend sat and just stared at it.

Andy looked at me and said, "if you need to do it to bring our girl back home safely then do it."

In my past, I was a person that people called when they wanted people to disappear and when they wanted no trace or trail to lead back to them. I was good at it too, damn good but I got caught up in it and let it consume me. I have been out of that life for a few years and putting my money where it is needed. I have known Andy since school, and we have always been close. I would trust him with my life, and I had trusted him with my secrets, he has never uttered a word. As I was fixing to touch the mamba Leon walked into the room.

"We may have found her." Leon said

Chapter 15(Sarah)

I had drifted off exhausted from the tears and not being able to move. I woke up to a seemingly dark room. There was a fire in the fireplace and the flames were dancing on the walls. I heard the creaking outside the door and the sounding of pots and pans. I let out a breath that I didn't know I was holding. Laying there, my body hurting to the point of numbness; I am past pain. My face was throbbing from my jaws, and I knew my face was bruised. Jesus, I thought I would never have to experience this again. Stinging tears were rolling down my cheeks. I heard footsteps and I tried to shake myself even though it hurt. I did not want Jade to see me in pain.

Jade came in with a tray of food; my stomach growled. To hear my stomach growl was betrayal to me. Jade standing there grinning a Joker's grin in the dark. She sat the tray down and walked over to the bed. I could tell that she had something in her hand. She reached for the bedside table light, blinding me. I closed my eyes and slowly turned away from the light. I adjusted, turned back to Jade and saw that in her hand was a dog's shock collar. She smiled and leaned in while placing the collar around my neck.

Jade then whispered in my ear.

"You won't be able to get away from me now."

I really didn't know how long I had been there; at this point every inch of my body hurt. I could tell my face was swollen and bruised. After she placed the collar on me, she leaned back and admired the collar.

"I am going to untie your arms and legs one at a time but if you try anything I am using the collar."

She started with my left arm and when she untied it my wrists were bleeding. There was an instant pain that washed over me from being in that position so long. One by one she untied the ropes, and it was like I was thrown into the fire. Every limb and every muscle in my body screamed in agony. It hurt to cry, it hurt to move.

My hope was failing me because I thought I was stronger than this. I thought I had gotten away from Jade. I had given myself hope of moving on and being happy. In that moment, Lavonna flashed into my mind. It was like a spark ignited but was soon snuffed out by doubt. I didn't even know Lavonna, and why anyone in their right mind invite this(me) into their life.

Even though doubt snuffed out the flame, there are embers burning and those embers can ignite again. I closed my eyes and focused on the pain.

 I told myself that *if there was pain, I was alive and if I was alive there was hope.*

And if I had hope I could get out of this with all my limbs attached hopefully. I was not going out defeated by the likes of Jade. I would leave this fucking cruel world kicking and fucking screaming.

I let my emotions wash over me feeling every one of them and then after I had gone through every emotion, I locked my emotions and placed them deep inside of me. I learned through pain that in dealing with Jade, I had to take the emotions out of the equation. She had always been two steps ahead of me even when I thought I was the one calling the shots. I let the last tears fall as I opened my eyes and looked at Jade fumbling with a chain. She hooked the chain to a metal loop that was lodged into the fireplace. She hooked a lock and chain to the collar I wore.

"I am still trying to figure out a lot of things Sarah. It looks like we will be here for a while. I am going to sort out what I want from you and decide if I even want you anymore. I need to see if you are truly sorry for leaving and cheating on me."

I started to open my mouth, but I stayed silent. The only way out was to feed Jade's delusions and play along until I could come up with a plan. I couldn't be too hasty because she would know it is all an act, so I chose silence. Yeah, that was my best option right now. At this point I only felt the pain in my body, and I knew I was dehydrated because when I tried to speak it came out as a squeak.

"Would it be possible to get some water or even maybe some pain meds?" I asked, trying to play Jade's emotions.

She looked at me and thought about it and her gaze started at the top of my head slowly taking my body in like it was the first time seeing all the damage to my wrist and legs, my swollen face.

"Yes, I will get you some. I will be right back."

She walked out and closed the door. I heard a click, which means there was a lock on the outside of the door. I made a mental note about that and filed that away for future reference. I slowly started trying to move my legs and arms and pain flooded my body. I knew it was going to take me a while to heal but I had to push through the pain and work on everything because when I had a chance, I had to take it. With Jade, I couldn't be hasty, or I may end up losing my life.

I heard Jade unlock the door from the outside. She came in with water and a bottle of Tylenol. I didn't think she would poison me at this point so I ate the soup and took the pain meds thinking maybe they would help some. I had gained some feeling back but sometimes it is better to feel numb. Jade sat in the leather chair by the fireplace watching me.

"So, I will let you rest tonight but tomorrow you will be explaining yourself and we will see what your future holds."

With that she got up walked out and locked the door.

Chapter 16(Lavonna)

We were standing around my dinner table with maps and documents scattered trying to come up with a plan for getting Sarah away from Jade. We finally narrowed it down to two houses within a five-mile radius. We had people watching both houses, but it was nightfall, and I was getting anxious.

Sarah should be in my arms right now and I was trying to keep a level head. When it came to this woman I was always thrown off and no one had ever had that effect on me. With Sarah, I was like a snake drawn to their prey. I ran my hands through my hair and told everyone I was stepping out for a second.

I walked outside to the backyard and stared into the sky hearing the waterfall that plunged into the pool in the distance. I calmed down a little because I knew I had to get my head in the game to save Sarah. Jade was smart, she had covered her tracks very well; even my guys were having trouble. I now have all the information on Jade since she was born up until now at my fingertips. I have poured over pages and pages of information to build my defenses and proof my plan. Sarah will be free by tomorrow night. We couldn't move too rashly because we didn't know what Jade had up her sleeve and I wanted Sarah unharmed. I didn't let my mind think of the awful things that could be happening to her right now. I knew Jade was going to pay and this time she was going to pay with her life.

As I was forming ways to torture, Andy walked out holding a cup of coffee. I took the cup, inhaled the scent, and swallowed a sip. Andy and I stood there looking at the stars.

"I know that look in your eyes Lavonna and to be honest I was all for coming out here and trying to talk you off a ledge, but all I feel is anger toward Jade, and I want her to suffer. Sarah didn't tell you half of what this girl had put her through. She needs to pay Lavonnna," he said with anger.   He looked up at the stars trying to calm down. I sipped my coffee, and that evil smile crept up on my face.

"I intend to make her pay Andy---- I intend to." I replied.

We walked back into the dining room, and I looked at the map. I asked for the blueprints on both houses so we can be prepared for everything. We found the car that Jade was using. It was in between both houses, so we placed surveillance teams there. Not too close because we didn't want to underestimate Jade. By morning we should be able to nail down which house Sarah was being held in.

"Lavonna, you need to stay put." Leon said.

"Like hell I am, that is not up for discussion so let's move on." I said angrily.

Leon nodded and continued about our impending approach. Both houses had been rented out and both names had come back to different people. So, with this we knew Jade was using an alias or had stolen someone's identity.

While we were pouring over ways to get in the house and make sure it wasn't booby trapped with extra surprises, my phone rang. It flashed, unknown number. I snatched it off the table and answered it.

"Well, hello there Ms. Lavonna Black, how is your evening going?"

It was Jade on the other end. I recognized her voice from some of the recordings we were able to pull from Sarah's phone.

"What do you want?" I said through gritted teeth.

"Oh, I wanted to chat woman to woman. Sarah is mine and she will always be mine. If you try anything or bring the police into this, she will be the one paying for your mistakes. I am going to break her physically and after that I will break her mentally. I want you to understand the severity of this Ms. Black" and in that instant my phone dinged in my ear.

I looked at my phone, it was a photo of Jade with a blade to Sarah's throat. It seemed that Sarah was sleeping but the way she was lying I could tell that was a lie.

"What the hell have you done to her and what did you give herrrr" I growled.

"Tsk Tsk Ms. Black, now that is nothing to worry your pretty little head about. She has only been given sleeping pills; to sleep. But know that I am not afraid to show Sarah a little pain since she craves that so much." Jade ended with laughing.

Then the line went dead.

I screamed and went to throw the phone, and I stopped. I need that picture we need to analyze it to narrow down where Sarah could be. It was dark in the picture, but I could see the faint glow, maybe a fireplace. Sarah had something around her neck, but I couldn't tell what it was at first. I looked at the picture and it hit me, that is a fucking dog collar. I realized that it was a shock collar and there was a lock, and a chain attached to it.

My blood was fucking boiling at this point. *Sarah was mine; she was fucking mine and no one in this fucking world will lay a finger on her and get away with it. I would burn this whole god damn world and walk through the ashes to get to her.*

I had to come up with a plan but then doubt creeped in; what if Jade hurts her, what if she kills her. She was expecting something, or she wouldn't have called.

"Leon pull all the men back and leave one on each house. Have them change positions because she knows something. I don't know how she has gotten tipped off but have your best guy sweep that car and around it. We missed something and it is giving her the advantage."

Leon walked out already speaking on the phone with someone. I stood there looking down at everything on the table with Andy standing beside me.

She is making her move and I am not sure if we will be able to move, is this checkmate I asked out loud to no one in particular.

Chapter 17(Sarah)

I woke up and my body felt twice as bad as yesterday. I didn't think I would be able to endure this pain forever. *When did I fall asleep?* I looked around the room and it was still dark. It is very unusual for a bedroom not to have a window. Then I saw it, a sliver of light. It wasn't much but with the room in utter darkness I could see it behind where there was a big picture hanging.

My mouth was so dry, and I felt the comings of a migraine, but I couldn't let that stop me. I slowly started moving toward the side of the bed. With every movement my body ached and protested in pain. I was going to push through. I had to play into Jades's hands and feed her delusions if I ever wanted to make it out alive. I got my feet planted on the floor and pain flooded my body. It took a couple of time trying to stand up, but I was pushing through; dammit this would not be the end. I listened and heard no noises from the outside of the room. I didn't want to get caught. I walked to where the painting was and right when I leaned in, I heard footsteps.

I made my way back to bed as quietly as possible. I was sitting on the edge when Jade opened the door and looked at me smiling a Joker's smile.

"Well, well well, look who is up and about."

I tried placing a real smile on my face even though my jaws hurt from the bruises, and it looked a little lopsided. I did not speak, thinking silence was the best course of action. My mouth ran away from me a lot. Jade had her back turned to me and set the tray of food down. I saw the keys hooked to her jeans. Fuck it, I wasn't going to wait until Jade lost all her marbles. I lunged for the keys knocking us both to the ground. I had my hand on the keys, and I was trying to pull them off her pants. It took

Jade a second to get her bearings as I grabbed the tray and hit her with it. She rolled over and grabbed the remote to the shock collar and pressed the button. Instant shock and pain had me grasping for the collar. I dropped to the ground in the fetal position with tears streaming down my face. I was clawing at the collar; I just wanted the pain to stop.

Who would ever put this on any animal that they loved?

Jade was standing over me laughing. I looked up to her through blurry eyes from the tears and the fucking pain.

Jade screamed at me, "you like that huh, you fucking like that."

She finally stopped pressing the button and I rolled over. It was not pretty;

everything hurt. I just lay there then she hit the button again only for a few seconds, I screamed wordlessly. She stopped, sat in the chair, and put her face in her hands.

"Why do you make me do this, whyyyyy" she screamed.

She picked up the tray and threw it across the room.

"I just don't know Sarah I just don't know." Jade kept repeating.

She left me lying curled up on the floor and walked out and as the door slammed, I heard the lock click back in place. I cursed myself. Sarah how can you be so fucking stupid I reacted to soon without a plan. For now, my neck hurt like a motherfucker and my whole body felt tingly. I tried to crawl back to bed but I couldn't move. I had to think but I was getting delirious, so I had to slow down. Jade would be gone for a while, and I knew I needed to explore what I could. I could barely move so I needed to rest if only for a second.

Now I understand what my doctor once told me about being sleep deprived and exhausted; it will have you making bad decisions. As I lay there, I heard the front door shut, I knew she wouldn't be far but for right now I was going to rest. I lay curled up on the floor with the last of the dying embers in the fireplace and let the sleep pull me under.

I heard footsteps on the stairs coming toward the bedroom as I woke. Still a little groggy with my eyes trying to focus as the light of the fire had long been extinguished. I wondered how long I had been out. I couldn't see but a tiny very tiny sliver of light from behind the picture. Whether it was night or day or how long I had been there it seemed like ages but there was no way to tell. The lock clicked and the light from the door blinded me when it came flooding in. I tried to shield my eyes and all I seen was spots.

Jade had walked in holding a few roses. I have always loved flowers, especially red roses. Jade tried to look so innocent, but my first thought was to spit in her face when she leaned down holding the roses. She twirled them in her fingers, missing the thorns that were still attached to them. She extended the freshly cut roses for me to inhale the scent. She stood over me looking at the roses and started pulling each petal off one by one and dropping them on me. She looked like she was mesmerized. She grinned and stared down at me.

"She loves me, she loves me not" with each petal that was falling to the floor. "You know what Sarah the saying makes so much sense now."

I croaked out, "what saying."

I didn't even sound like me. My voice cracked and weak. She had pulled all the petals off and left with a single rose. I had pulled myself up leaning on my hands. She leaned down looking me straight in the face and glided the rose over my cheeks down to my jaw. That action from Jade gave me chills. It was the type to make your stomach turn from being sick. She leaned in so close and breathed.

"Even beautiful things can hurt us" and with that, she raked the rose across my cheek with the thorns.

I felt the pain immediately and as the blood started dripping from my face, she stood up, dropped the rose and walked out of the door. The last thing I heard was the lock click in place.

Chapter 18(Lavonna)

I am done waiting. Who the fuck does Jade think she is? I am Lavonna Black, the serpent in the dark. I may not be known by my name, but I am the Black Mamba in other circles. I smiled when I thought of Sarah's safe word as if she knew what I was. If she did, would she still want me? I have killed countless times without any emotion. Would she cower at me or leave me if I told her my deepest darkest secrets. Leon walked up to me snapping me out of thought. This woman has my mind wrapped up; I must fucking shake this. I looked at Leon expecting an update.

"I know that look Lavonna" Leon said, and he handed me my bag.

I took it from him, laid it on the ground and brushed my hand over the soft leather. There was a black mamba sketched into the leather. I was feeling the coarseness of the snake, and I felt myself go numb. Jade dies today or maybe I will make it a slow and painful death. I opened the case, placed the black gloves on, took the knives out and one by one ran them through the venom of an actual black mamba. That is where I got the name. Anyone that got cut by my knives only had thirty to forty-five minutes if they didn't struggle. I kept the antidote close to my heart and without it my victims would die. A black mamba's name comes from the insides of their mouth being black. They are also fast and aggressive.

"Pull the men back to observe I am going in myself."

Before Leon could protest, I held up my hand.

"There is no saving Jade she was doomed when she took Sarah, she just didn't know it yet."

I looked at Leon "Make sure the doctor is on standby just in case."

With that I walked into the woods to blend in with the darkness that slowly enveloped me. We have narrowed it down to two houses and I am done with waiting. I went to the car that was nestled deep in between the two houses. I walked slowly around the area and noticed that there were trip wires around the vehicle. I side stepped and kept my eye on the area. Jade may be crazy, but she is not dumb. I scanned the area as I knelt beside the car. I pulled one of the knives out and punctured two of the tires. I moved past the trip wires headed to the first house. I heard Leon's voice come through my ear.

"We have figured out what house it is."

Then everything went silent. I touched the earpiece.

"Leon Leon, can you hear me." I asked.

Awe that means she has a jammer that is blocking all electronics. I will have to work faster. I was nearing the first house and there were a couple of lights on, one upstairs and one downstairs, was this the house? I slid myself up next to the wall trying to listen and I heard a tv. Something felt off but I couldn't put my finger on it. I made my way to the side of the house looking for trip wires or any indication that this was it when I came to a storm door that led into the basement. Seeing a lock on it. I leaned down and took my lock pickers out of my pocket. It took me ten seconds to get the lock undone. I am getting out of practice even though I don't use these skills anymore. I may need to still practice them I thought because I have gotten too comfortable that is the reason Jade got the jump on me. Anger flared inside of me for a second, but I quickly snuffed that flame out. I cannot have emotions involved but when it came to Sarah, from the moment I saw her I knew she was going to be mine.

I was like a moth to the flame and Sarah was the flame, but I would fly straight through that fire to set the whole world ablaze and watch it burn to make sure she was safe. That is the difference between heroes and villains. You see heroes will sacrifice the people they love for the greater good, but villains will go to the end of the world for the person they love. We grow up thinking we want to be saved by the hero but when we are grown, we see the villains in a whole new light. No one and I mean no one messes with what is mine. I eased the storm door open and slipped into the darkness of the basement. I let my eyes adjust to the pitch darkness while relying on other senses. I heard what sounded like a tv but other than that I did not hear any other movement.

I slowly crept up the stairs stopping in place when the stairs beneath me groaned under the weight of being used. Still nothing, it was quiet a little too quiet for my taste. I felt something, I lowered myself to see if I could see movement under the door and there was nothing but the tv in the background. I did see something that looked as if it was aimed at the front door. So, we may have something rigged for this door as well. I looked at the stairs and noticed that they were angled down. I tried the knob and when it turned, I saw that it was unlocked. I knew there was a trap waiting for me on the other side.

I remember seeing duct tape when I slipped into the window. I made my way quietly down the stairs. I grabbed the duct tape and made a handle to go around the doorknob and let a piece hang all the way down so while I laid on the stairs I could open the door. The stairs had no railing on the left side so if I needed to roll off the stairs. I made sure there would be nothing that sliced me up in the process but really hoping whatever trapped is aimed for someone's head or heart so if laid on the stairs it will miss me entirely.

I positioned the makeshift handle on the knob and lowered myself to the floor. I blended into the darkness. Ok here goes nothing, I pulled the tape, and it twisted the door open. As the door swung open, I saw the bow and the three arrows fly past me and connect with the wall. I looked and rolled out of the doorway. I surveyed everything and it looked like there was a sawed-off shotgun trained on the front door and more arrows trained on the basement door. The only other door was the kitchen door and there was an axe waiting for when that door was opened.

Hum, these were easy traps that would have either did great damage or killed someone if they had no expertise and that was what Jade was expecting. I had hidden my past very well. Not even powerful people could get my information. Jade was sloppy but strategic. Sometimes being unpredictable is the worst because they have nothing to lose and when someone is backed into a corner and fighting for their life something else completely takes over.

I went upstairs and none of the bedrooms were being used. This was the decoy house I now knew that Jade and Sarah were in the other house. I made it to the kitchen and there was a burner phone lying on the counter. As soon as I looked at the phone it started to ring. The note beside it said, "Good Job you are not dead answer me." I clicked the line open for Leon hoping they had taken care of the jammer by now. I put the phone on speaker and Jade's laughter came over the phone.

"Well, well Ms. Black it seems like I have underestimated you. I thought you to be a spoiled fucking rich woman that wouldn't get her hands dirty. You are more than meets the eye. Since you are still alive, and you obviously can have any woman you want let us call this a draw and you go back to your life and forget about Sarah. She is just a grain of sand on a whole beach. She is nothing special to you just another notch on your bedpost."

Anger was bubbling at this bitch calling Sarah nothing special. But I stayed calm and scanned the kitchen. I saw the red lights flashing in the foyer. Jade had been watching and observing me the whole time. The cameras were hidden rather good. That is how she knew to call when I got to the kitchen. The question I didn't know is which way to go with Jade. Do I pretend to give in, or do I intentionally make her mad?

Jade was in a craze right now and either way could make this go bad.

"So, you just want me to walk out of here and go on with my life. Okay then Jade, a life for a life. I leave and you take Sarah home." I replied.

"Yes, that is what I am offering this has gone on way too long and Sarah doesn't want you anyway. She has made her decision so leave her be Lavonna. You are the one that is bothering us now. Ms. Black can you not take rejection. Sarah told me she was scared and wanted to come home so just leave us alone."

"Fine, I will pull back. Just let me hear that from Sarah and I will walk out of these woods pull all my men back and be done." I said as I threw my hands in the air.

I heard muffling and moving around and if you weren't listening to the background, you wouldn't have heard the faint click before Sarah's voice came through the phone.

"I don't want Ms. Black. We can go home and build a life together." Sarah said.

Then I heard Jade through the phone.

"You see she wants me not you so take your loss and leave us the fuck alone."

I had a moment to decide which way to go and I was going to lean into her delusions.

"Okay Jade, I see I have lost, and I threw my hands up. I will leave and we can call it a draw. You and Sarah go on with your life and I will go on with mine. I am going to go ahead and leave."

I looked around and slipped the phone in my pocket. I knew Jade would see it and would track it. I dismantled the traps so no one would intentionally get hurt with her games. I went out the front door and walked into the darkness of woods. I walked to Leon and looked at my pocket so he would know I still had the phone.

"Let's move out and call it; we are going home."

Leon touched his comms and told everyone to fall back, we are calling it. Leon and I got into the back of the SUV. I texted on the phone not sure if Jade had the phone bugged or not, I took the phone out and sat it in the seat next to us.

I texted and told Leon *Send everyone home and keep the phone on you all the way home. Take the phone inside the house and walk around with it to make sure it is always moving. About a mile out slow down, there is a curve but don't stop it will show that we stopped. I am going to jump from the car and go back for Sarah.*

Leon had already sent me the layout of the house we knew she was in. Jade is going to be watching that phone. I told him to make sure he forwarded the call to me so I could answer. I knew Jade was going to call because she operates in paranoia. He nodded and about a mile down they slowed down enough for me to jump and roll out of the car.

I told Leon to let me know when they made it back to the house because Jade would call then. I started making my way back to the house. Regardless of what I heard and even though I knew that was Sarah's voice, I couldn't let that sway me because I heard the recorder click. Sarah is in survival mode and Jade is taking advantage of that. *I am coming my little dragonfly.*

Chapter 19 (Sarah)

I didn't know how long I had been there lying in complete darkness and I didn't know whether it was day or night. My body is still reeling from the pain. I had to push through if I wanted to get out of here alive. So, I kept telling myself don't give up.

I heard footsteps coming toward the bedroom. The lock clicking signaling that freedom was just beyond that door sucks. I never learned how to pick locks I thought as Jade entered the room with a tray of food and a medical kit. Hum I may be able to work this to my advantage. Jade thought she had broken me and made me docile like before. I was not that woman anymore, but I may need to pretend enough for Jade to believe it.

I was still laying on the floor next to the rose that Jade had dropped. The petals had started to wither and die kinda ironic I thought to myself. We are like roses, we are beautiful when we bloom but if not taken care of or plucked, we start withering and dying. When this happens, no amount of care can bring us back to the vibrancy before being plucked from our roots.

I looked at Jade and tried to sit up. I let out a groan because my ribs were in so much pain, among other things. Jade sat the tray down and helped me to my feet. My blood ran cold where she touched me, I wanted to recoil but she just thought it was from the pain. She slowly guided me to the chair in front of the fireplace. Jade still had not said a word. She pulled up the other chair and started to feed me the soup that was on the tray.

"Eat Sarah, your body needs nourishment."

Looking at Jade she looked so innocent and the look in her eyes pretending to care that was what made me fall for Jade. She listened to everything and found what I craved and used it against me. I now know she was doing that to get me hooked and trained to be her ever loving devoted Lil plaything that she could manipulate at will.

I let Jade feed me because I was still chained with the collar. It was beginning to cut into my neck. After feeding me the soup she got up and went to the bathroom. I heard water running. I leaned back in the chair to see if I was going to make Jade really believe I was back under her spell. I had to honestly play the long game.

I have gone back and forth about this. I am not giving in, or do I need to give in. I heard Jade walking back to the chair. I was still at war with myself when Jade sat the bowl of warm water on the table. It looked like it had soap in it. She leaned down and placed a washcloth in the water.

"We need to get you cleaned up and dress all your wounds." Jade said.

The voice inside of my head screaming what the fuck are you doing this is your chance and it was starting to drown out the rational side. I looked at Jade on her knees and saw the keys hanging from her belt buckle. I started thinking this may be the only chance I had because the door was open and unlocked. I looked up as Jade started speaking and at first my mind was not hearing what she said. It was just screaming at me to act first. I heard Lavonna's name, and it stopped the screaming in my head. I looked at Jade with her head down soaking the cloth in the water then looking at me. I blinked.

"Did you hear what I said Sarah?" Jade asked me.

I stuttered out. "No, I am sorry my ears were ringing, and I could hardly hear you."

Jade huffed with an annoyed tone. Not wanting to make her angry I sat there looking at her waiting for her to respond. She started cleaning the cut on my face trying to carefully miss all the bruises.

"Lavonna Black has informed me that she would not stand in our way of happiness and that you were only something to pass the time with and she could care less about what happened to you." Jade said with a smirk.

There it was the look of pride on Jade's face, the look of triumph. Something in my stomach lurched.

Lavonna was looking for me, she really did care for me.

Jade would have not even brought her up with that look of triumph. Hope, I had fucking hope. She and Andy were coming I just had to hold on a little longer. I looked at Jade and started to raise my hand to her face and then pulled it back suddenly. I was making sure Jade noticed as I winced in pain.

"It is ok Sarah I don't want to hurt you we belong together, and we will make a life together after we leave this place" Jade said.

I was about to play the role of a lifetime. I am going to need an Oscar when I get out of here. This is survival, this is my life, and I will be damned to just let it go.

Jade looked at me and asked, "can I trust you?"

I slowly shook my head yes.

"We need to get you into fresh clothes and get your ribs bandaged. I need to tend to your neck so don't try anything; you will not get far."

She grabbed the keys and unlocked the shock collar that was around my neck. My instincts urged me to run but I knew I had to play this role because maybe I could make it out of the room, but I didn't know the layout of the house and with my injuries I knew I wouldn't make it. If I angered Jade, she may change her mind. After she took the collar off, I leaned back into the chair. I made no attempt to move. I let Jade wash my neck and tend to the cuts and bruises on my face.

"You need to strip Sarah" Jade spoke softly.

I looked at Jade and I saw the look of hunger in Jade's eyes. This chilled me to my core and left me shivering on the outside.

You must commit to this Sarah, I told myself you have endured worse.

I centered myself and looked up at Jade standing over me.

"I don't think I can do it on my own can you help" and the look of satisfaction on Jades face I knew she approved.

.

"I tell you what you don't need this shirt and since your ribs are probably bruised let me take care of this shirt" and at that moment she pulled a knife from her back.

I knew terror showed on my face and I couldn't stop it. I missed it. I never saw the knife that she must have had sheathed underneath her shirt. Jade towered over me coming closer to my pulse in my throat and my breath started to quicken. She brought the knife to my face. I sat back in the chair utterly still.

Had I misjudged? Did I make a wrong move, and it was lights out for me. I didn't see it coming.

Jade leaned into me, her face centimeters from mine. She trailed the knife down my cheek over my chin then gliding down my throat. I couldn't help but swallow when it glided down my throat.

"I thought you liked this kind of stuff Sarah it seems I have you at a loss for words." You don't need a safe word with me."

She glided the knife down the shirt between the breast and with every breath I took the pain was sharp, it was like inhaling needles.

"Hold still Sarah or I may cut youuuu" she cooed.

I don't think I breathed for what seemed like an eternity, she grabbed my shirt taking the knife and slicing all the way up my shirt. She stopped right at my chin. The realization that she just cut the shirt all the way up. She pulled back and sheathed the knife. I had grabbed both arms of the chair and I had a death grip on each arm.

"Now let's get you out of those clothes."

She helped pull one arm through the tattered fabric and it dropped to the floor. I stood there with only my bra and pants for comfort, but I looked at the bruises all up and down my ribs. Jade wrapped my bruised ribs, they are the worst because there is absolutely nothing you can do, I really hoped I didn't have any cracked or broken ones because I was realizing I was still in shock, and everything was wearing off and everything hurt. I could not make any movement that didn't hurt. I started to get sleepy, my eyes started to flutter shut.

"Oh, I see the painkillers I laced in the soup are starting to kick in."

She helped me to the bed and bent down and got on her knees in front of me she started unbuttoning my jeans and pulling them down. She sat me on the side of the bed. But before I could utter anything out of my mouth I passed out.

Chapter 20 (Lavonna)

I had made it about a half mile. I didn't want to get too close because I knew the call would come soon. Leon came through on my earpiece.

"Ms. Black we are in the house as requested and I have Vinny walking around with the phone. So, what is the plan exactly,"

At that moment I heard a branch break to my right. I swirled around ready to strike.

Leon said, "Andy is on his way, he should be making it to you soon."

Andy came from the bushes with his hands up. Looking at Andy in his face. I touched my earpiece.

"Leon why the fuck is Andy here?"

Andy grinned only because he could hear Leon in his ear just like I could. Leon sighed with so much tiredness in his voice.

"I am sorry Ms. Black, he took off as soon as he heard what happened, I looked around and he took my phone to locate where you were."

Before I could utter a word, Andy said,

"I don't want to fucking hear it, Lavonna; so, save it. I am going with you; Sarah is like a sister to me, and I am not going to stand idly by and lose her. I will not lose her you hear me."

I sighed because I knew there was no talking him down when he was like this.

"Andy, I don't want to lose you either and I don't know what we are walking into."

He looked at me and made a zipping gesture with his mouth when my phone started to vibrate. I pulled out the phone right on time. I knew her pride would not let her just leave. We were close to an abandoned shed that I saw on the map when I was looking at the area. I motioned Andy to the shed because it was quiet. I answered the phone and placed it on speaker.

"Hi Ms. Black, have you made it home yet?"

I heard the grin in Jade's voice thinking she was a move ahead of me.

"Yes, I have, and I have called all my men back. You and Sarah are free to leave and live your life." I replied.

"I knew you would see reason Ms. Black; you are a smart woman. Know I can always find you and I will know if you go back on your word." Jade said with a smile in her voice.

"I understand exactly, is there anything else?"

"No Ms. Black there is nothing else. Let me go now, Sarah kind of kept me up all night. I just wanted you to know how peaceful she looks when she is in my arms asleep." Jade started laughing and hung up.

Anger rolled through my body like hot lava. Andy started shaking me.

"Lavonna, you know she is trying to get under your skin."

"You're right let's go get Sarah." I said.

With Jade it was all about control and in chess you always want to be one step ahead of your opponent. But Jade didn't know that she would soon know what checkmate was really like.

Leon was in our ears once again,

"We found tracking devices on the trucks."

I looked at Andy as he said, "I used the hunting truck in the garage, so it doesn't stand out."

"I don't think she tracked the hunting truck. It seems to be limited to the main cars that sit out." Leon said.

"Leave the devices alone for now I want her to think she has the upper hand. We know that she had traps rigged on the other house so it is more than likely she will have traps on this house as well. We don't know what condition Sarah is in so have the doctor at the house Leon."

I looked at Andy pulling the blueprints up to the house. We went over entrances and exits and I filled him in on the traps that I had encountered at the previous house. I think she will try to move Sarah tonight. If Jade succeeds it will put us behind and we might lose Sarah forever and I am not willing to ever lose her. The sun would be setting soon, and the plan was for Andy and me to enter the house using separate entrances to get the jump on her. I hoped Andy was ready for what laid behind those doors. In this moment, I had to trust him.

We were walking up to the house, and I saw the trap before Andy did. I placed a hand on his shoulder and told him to freeze. He froze in that position. If he had taken one more step there was an axe waiting and it would have alerted Jade to us being outside. I followed the trip wire to the nearby tree and disabled it with Andy still frozen because his foot was touching the wire. He didn't want to offset it until I was able to disarm it. I signaled to him that he was good. He took a step over the wire and pointed to the ground in front of him where there was a silver glint under the leaves. He leaned toward it, and I made my way to him watching every step I took. I looked down, it was a bear trap. Hum she might would have taken some of my men down with these. I touched my ear and spoke very low.

"Did the guys find the trip wire and bear traps when they were doing surveillance?" I asked.

Leon came on the other end; I heard him speaking to some of the men and he came over the ear bud.

"No Ms. Black they did not."

I was seething not only were my men careless, but Jade could have killed some of them.

My voice was low almost at a growl.

"Retraining starts tomorrow. Leon these could have killed some of them or at least maimed them for life. These were careless mistakes."

"Understood Ms. Black," Leon responded in my ear.

I looked at Andy and we moved forward but we didn't find any more booby traps on the way to the house. Andy was going to take the side door that led from the dining room, but I was going through the fucking front door. I waited till Andy was in place. I leaned against the wall. I heard talking but it wasn't close. I chanced a look through the window. There was a staircase off to the right of the front door. I looked but it didn't look like the doors were holding surprises on the other side.

I took my lock picking tools out and had the door unlocked in nine seconds, *still too long* I scolded myself. I knew Andy would be fine on his end because we learned to pick locks when we were younger. I slipped the door open, and it didn't even creak. Thank God I saw Andy coming in from the back. I pointed upstairs where I heard Jades voice.

Jade's voice was elevating as both me and Andy moved slowly up the stairs. I pulled out the only knife that did not have the snake venom because I was not done with Jade by a longshot. She had torture in her future and boy was I good at torture. I felt the evil grin creep on my face and all my emotions slipping into darkness when I was completing a mission. This mission was personal because Sarah was for keeps. Jades voice started getting clearer with the distance closing. We made it to the top of the stairs. The door at the end of the hallway had a lock on the outside. It must have been the master bedroom and where Jade was holding Sarah.

I heard Jade screaming at Sarah telling her that she would have to tough through the pain that they were leaving. She told Sarah that she would have to walk on her own and maybe if she hadn't gotten so fucking fat, she could have carried her. Rage was instantly there because I loved every inch of Sarah's body. She was a beautiful goddess.

Andy and I made it to the end of the hallway. He was on the left and I was on the right. Andy twisted the knob. I was ready to take the room and strike as soon as he opened the door. He threw the door open.

I saw Jade standing there with her gun pointing at Sarah. I tackled Jade and after a brief struggle I had her in a choke hold. I had one hand around her neck and the other hand holding the gun pinned against the wall. Jade reacted quite fast knocking me into the wall. We both fell against the fireplace bricks, at this point I had to release her hand. She pointed the gun at Andy and fired. Thankfully, he rolled out of the way. I twirled Jade around and punched her hard. It unsteadied her enough for me to kick the gun from her hands. The gun went skidding under the bed.

I made the mistake of taking my eyes off Jade for a split second. She came up with a fire poker and swung. Andy rushed her, she kicked him in the balls, and I watched him drop to his knees. As Andy tried to regain his composer, I started to get off the floor. Getting up wasn't quite that easy because Jade was swinging the fire poker down at me. I knew this was going to hurt. Just as she was about to connect, Sarah lunged at Jades feet and made Jade fall next to the bed. I got up and started across the room. Jade rolled over and pointed the gun at me. She was breathing heavily; she had pulled the gun from under the bed. Sarah was on her knees struggling to get up, but Jade pointed the gun at me and Andy.

"Don't come any closer." She screamed.

We stopped moving and watched as she backhanded Sarah and called her a fucking bitch. Sarah hit the floor and didn't move. I moved and when Jade shot the bullet whizzed over my head. I rushed her again and after a struggle I took the gun from her. Andy tackled Jade to the floor riding her all the way down.

"I got Jade handled check on Sarah."

He was pulling out standard issued cop handcuffs that Leon had given him. He had Jade pinned. I ran over to Sarah where she lay crumpled on the floor. I pulled her into my lap not wanting to hurt her. I looked closely at Sarah and noticed all the bruises on her face and the blood starting to run from her cracked lip.

"Sarah, baby," I called.

She slowly opened her eyes as if she was trying to focus. She lifted her hand to my face and cupped it.

"I knew you would come" it was barely above a whisper and then her hand fell; she passed out.

Chapter 21 (Sarah)

I woke up in darkness. There was only a sliver of light from what I think was a bathroom. My body felt like I had run into oncoming traffic with a bus and lost. Panic immediately set in. I felt a warm presence next to me. I went rigid and my arm felt heavy when I tried to move the covers. I saw the IV in my arm.

More panic set in, *was I being drugged what happened where am I?*

Then it all came rushing back to me. Lavonna and Andy bursting in the door. The figure beside me stirred, Lavonna rolled over to turn on the lamp by the bedside table and rolled back to face me.

"How are you feeling baby?" she asked.

Her fucking voice tightening things lower, and I know I frowned. Like how in the hell is my body reacting like this when I feel like I got put through a meat grinder.

"Why are you frowning sweetheart?

I shook my head, and I realized I shouldn't have done that. Everything hurt and it made me dizzy. Lavonna set up and placed her hand on my face.

"Gently baby be careful you are still healing, and you are probably hurting like a son of a bitch right now. The doctor bandaged up everything. You do have bruised ribs among other things, so you need rest. I will make sure you get that. You are safe!!" Lavonna said.

Then instant dread hit me. I tried to speak but my mouth was so dry. I licked my lips and swallowed. My mouth felt like I had been licking sand.

I squeaked out, "what about Jade?"

Lavonna rolled off the bed and walked around to my side. On the dresser was a water pitcher, she poured some in a glass and walked over to me. She helped me lift my head and let me drink and omg that water was everything.

"She will not be hurting anyone anymore we will discuss it when you get a little better. For now, Nurse Lavonna is reporting for duty."

She leaned in and whispered in my ear "you better take advantage of this because I wouldn't do this for anyone but you."

She waggled her eyebrows at me, I snickered, and it hurt a lot.

"Rest sweetness I am going to get you something to eat and let Andy know you are awake. He hasn't left the house and is driving me up the wall."

"How long have I been out," I asked.

"Three days, but your body needed the rest."

She leaned in and kissed me on my forehead and whispered, "you are safe now baby and I am never letting you go."

With that she walked out of the room humming. Not as soon as Lavonna walked out, Andy came running in. He ran to the bed and started to try and pull me into a hug but realized and stopped.

"I am okay," I squeaked.

I could tell he hadn't shaved, and he looked like he hadn't slept either.

"Awe look at the most eligible Bachelor in town worried about Lil o me."

He chuckled and pulled up a chair to the bed.

"I was so worried; don't you go giving me gray hairs before my time."

He took my hand and held it. I looked at him and I said, "thank you."

"Sarah, you have become my best friend I will always be here for you." he replied.

He leaned in and rested his head on mine ever so softly.

"Don't scare me like that anymore Sarah, I am glad you are okay."

I was so thankful I had made such a great friend. People would kill for these types of friends. Lavonna walked in carrying a tray.

"Hey now don't be putting the moves on my woman. I can't leave you alone for one minute."

"I am your woman" I asked

"Yes ma'am you are forever and always."

Lavonna replied with a smile.

Chapter 22 (Lavonna)

I made my way down the winding staircase

to the basement. It has been four years since

I came down here. I thought I would never use or spill blood in this room ever again but the blood this time will be the last time. I pushed open the heavy metal door and it creaked on its hinges opening. It was pitch black and had a dampness that you could feel in your bones. I flipped on the lights; Jade was sitting there in the middle of the floor strapped to the chair slumped over.

She blinked fast, trying to adjust to the harshness of the light. Instant fear came over her face.

"Just kill me and get it over with" she screamed.

"No, that would be too easy of a punishment for you. You will suffer the way you have made Sarah suffer for years but yours will be in days. You will beg for your death, but I will not give it to you until I'm ready. This is the end of the road for you but before then you will endure pain, and I want to hear you beg me for death. I want to hear your cries and see the pain on your face replaced by despair. I could hear you over and over again and it wouldn't be enough. Do you see what your crazy has gotten you into. These hands are much crazier than yours. You should have let Sarah go but no you had to keep on coming." I replied walking up to Jade.

"Does Sarah know what you do in the dark Miss Black" she spat those words at me.

"Sarah will not love you the way she loves me, especially this side of you."

I laughed; "Sarah loves every part of me. Jade, the difference between you and I is that you want to control her, and I want to protect her. I am the villain of the story and as the villain I must live up to it. Where you want her to be a pawn in your chess game for your own amusement, that is the difference between me and you. She gives herself willingly to me, she shows me the darkest parts of her, and I will show her the darkest parts of me."

I pulled out the knife that was in my thigh sheath. It shined in the harsh lights of the basement; Jades eyes went wide.

"Now it's time to have a little something I call fun."

I walked toward her and brought the blade up to her face.

"I wonder how many cuts you can take before you start begging." I said.

"I will not fucking beg" Jade said and spit at me.

My laugh was so evil "ohh is that so. I look forward to breaking you."

A slice downward on her cheek and a thin line of red Crimson came to the surface. Then I moved to the other side of her face. Another slice downward and Jades eyes were still defiant. She didn't know what she was in for. The next hour I made small cuts all over her body not enough for stitches but enough to bleed like small paper cuts where every time she moved it hurt. I made these cuts all down her arms, her torso, and her legs. I wiped off the blade on her clothes and walked out.

"That's all for today, we'll pick up tomorrow where we left off."

I flipped the lights off and closed the door. As I walked up the stairs, I did wonder whether Sarah would accept who I am. As soon as she gets better, I will tell her. I will let her know Lavonna Black in every form and let her decide. But in her decision, she will never be free of me. Jade did have one thing right when something is mine, it will always be mine. Sarah has etched herself into my brain and since I've had a taste of her, I will never let her go.

Chapter 23(Sarah)

I was starting to feel better, the doctor kept telling me not to push myself and to take it easy, but I was going crazy sitting and laying in this bed day after day. I still was sore but that wasn't going to go away overnight. It had been ten whole days, and I wanted sunshine on my face. I wanted to get back to normal as quickly as possible. Andy and Lavonna were both driving me insane. I couldn't move without one of them running to help me. I felt like a porcelain doll. I chuckled to myself; it is nice to be catered to. It was nice to see Lavonna get so flustered over little stuff. She always slept with me at night now, but she would sneak in late. She thought I was asleep and tried to be so quiet, but I was always awake. I only pretended to be asleep.

I asked Andy and Lavonna about Jade several times and they immediately changed the conversation. I needed some answers, and I was going to get some but first I was going to relieve some stress, if you know what I mean. Every fucking night I must lay in bed next to this Goddess of a woman; I felt like a limp noodle. Luckily today Andy said he was busy at the shop and Lavonna would be in meetings all day.

Lavonna said she had to take care of a couple of things, so this is my first day officially on my own. I knew I wasn't technically on my own with Leon and Luna, but this is my sanctuary today and I was fixing to give myself an offering my body has been begging for.

Closing my eyes and letting my hands wander along my body stopping at my breast kneading them. I reached for my phone to pull up a flick to watch but I wanted something else. Let's see what my mind can envision. I do have a very active imagination. I closed my eyes again and at first all I saw was darkness but then I relaxed letting my hands flow over my body.

I found myself in front of Lavonna's study. I knocked on the door and there was no answer. Seeing the light shining from the lamp. I knew she was in there, so I opened the door and walked towards the desk. Her chair was turned backwards; she was on the phone with someone. I walked over to her. I could tell it was an important call but oh how I wanted her. I wanted her right now. She turned in her chair and almost dropped the phone. I have wanted her forever. I walked toward her and started to slowly unbutton each button on her shirt. She watched as I did it. I got on my knees while taking her jacket off. She moved the phone to the other hand to help me take off her jacket. I am staring up at her and then I trail my eyes down her body. I see a peek of her bra underneath, it's a black bra ohh my God. Her skin was so fucking smooth. I got up off my knees and started kissing her on her neck.

I worked my way down from her breast to her belly button. I got back on my knees and did a little lick up her stomach. I can tell she wants me because she is taking deep breaths while still on the phone. Finally, she had enough and told whoever was on the phone that she would have to call him back.

She threw the phone down on the desk, grabbed my face and pulled me to her. She starts kissing me harshly, but I stopped her shaking my head. I put my finger on her lips and said no this time I am gonna please you. She places her hands on my hips and tries to start moving my body I take her hands off and place them on each side of the chair. I got up and waggled my finger no no.

I watch as she's still had her pants on. I unbuttoned her collared shirt and took in the sight as I let my lustful gaze look at her. I stepped back and dropped my red satin nightgown to the floor leaving me in nothing but black and red bottomed heels. She squeezed the arms of the chair; I can tell she is fighting not to get up and take control.

I leaned in and whispered in her ear, "don't move" as I started trailing kisses from her neck all the way down. My hands go to her breast kneading and pinching her nipples through the fabric of the bra. I put both hands on her shoulders and slipped her out of her other shirt.

Lavonna is just looking at me. I looked in her eyes and saw pure desire and fire. I start unbuckling her pants and slowly trailing her body with kisses.

I speak in a whisper, "help me with the pants."

She lifted a little bit so I could take her pants and panties off. That just leaves her with the bra. God, she is so fucking gorgeous. I take my nails and slide them over her breast down her stomach all the way to her thighs. I want to know what she tastes like. I pulled her to the edge of the seat, the leather giving way underneath her. I nibble her thighs going inward. My hands found her breast my mouth getting closer to her pussy. I could feel the heat before I made it to her folds. My lips feeling she was wet and the heat that was coming off her let me know she wanted me, and I wanted and craved her. I kiss each one of her lips, my mouth coming away glistening. Looking at her while still on my knees. I push her legs apart pulling her folds back. She was so wettt, do I get this wet? I felt myself starting to drip.

I plunged into her wetness I wanted it to coat my tongue and if it coats my face too that would be amazing. I could feel her breath deepening as I got into a rhythm. I explored and teased a little to get reactions out of her and to find out how she likes it.

Every woman's body is different. Finding that sweet spot, I quickened my pace. Ohh she tastes so fucking good, almost sweet like pineapples. She was getting close because she grabbed a headful of my hair and pushed me into her pussy further. I could hardly breathe but I didn't care to breathe I just wanted to please her. I want her to cum for me and have my name on her lips when she does. I quicken the pace, her hand in my hair gets heavier and heavier. She starts pushing, she's almost there and then I feel it. Ohh I feel the wave riding her as she lets out a quick moan. I want her to have the ecstasy that she gives me, I want her legs shaking.

Her grip loosens and she tells me I am a good girl. She pulls me up and kisses me after that. She was up on her feet pushing me to the desk. Picking me up and putting me on the desk. She raised my legs trailing kisses with her hands playing between my thighs. Her lips on my lips kissing me passionately as her fingers slid between my pussy.

Lavonna groaned "Oh my God you're like a fucking ocean. Why are you always so wet?"

Then she plunged her fingers inside me. Ohh, I exhaled and took a deep breath at the initial shock of her velvety fingers. She fucked me with her fingers while her tongue assaulted my mouth. She makes her way down pulling her fingers and places them in my mouth.

 "I wanna see you suck them clean Sweetness."

So, as I sucked them Lavonna's got on her knees and started kissing on my pussy opening. That first lick almost brought me to the edge. She sucked my clit into her mouth, and she knew exactly where to lick. I was on the edge of my orgasm when she hit that spot and brought me to my brink screaming her name. I came back to reality and heard myself screaming her name in real life because that was the best orgasm ever. I pulled my fingers from between my pussy because I wanted to taste myself.

Closing my eyes and placing my fingers in my mouth licking them clean. After that I lay panting on the bed. My arms laid out to the side trying to learn how to breathe again. Today was going to be a good day, a weight lifted off my shoulders.

I did have a nagging sensation about why Andy and Lavonna were avoiding the topic of Jade. I needed to know to be able to close that chapter. I would get answers tonight from Lavonna whether I had to stay up till dawn.

Chapter 24 (Lavonna)

It had been a taxing day. I leaned back in my office chair and rubbed my temples. I was beginning to have a headache behind my eyes. I wondered if Sarah was asleep already. Today was the first time since I got Sarah back that she has not been within ear distance. I know she is cared for and seeing her I know she is stronger than she lets on.

When the doctor came out of the room, he was amazed that she was still alive. I still had Jade in the basement and every night after work I would go down and show her a new form of torture.

I was looking forward to tonight. I wanted to try something new, and I felt the evil grin spread on my face. I laid back in my black leather chair that was so comfortable it was like being engulfed in a pillow. With my eyes closed, my thoughts flowed back to Sarah and the picture of her naked underneath me. Sarah did not give herself enough credit, she was gorgeous. Her red hair reminded me of Jessica rabbit. She had an hourglass figure even though she thought she was too big, but I just loved the plushness, and her skin was so soft as I trailed my hands over her body. The tattoos that she has I didn't even know she had till she was standing in front of me naked just makes her more of an art piece than she already is. I growled because I put myself in a mood and I wanted her in the worst way.

Fuck, I needed her body to heal. I ran my hand through my hair and let out a growl of frustration. Let me get home, I got a person that was waiting for me to take out all my anger on. I had to stop in and check on my girl. I get increasingly nervous because I know that I am going to have to tell Sarah about Jade.

Andy and I have been avoiding and changing the subject, but I know that is drawing to a close. I got home and wanted something quick to munch on. I went to the kitchen and there was a plate and a note beside it telling me that she knew I had been busy and needed to eat something.

So, she is starting to get up and around.

I picked up the blt and took it to Andy's room. He had moved in since getting Sarah back. Sarah was beginning to steal him away from me, but I didn't mind because I loved them both! I knocked on Andy's door and he told me to come in. I was still eating the sandwich when I strolled in.

"Oh, I see you found the food Sarah left for you. You know she waited for you to come home and checked her phone every two seconds," Andy said.

Damn, I had gotten so caught up in my day and didn't even say anything to her. I will not let that happen again. I want to show her that she is a priority as I looked at Andy.

I finished the sandwich. Andy was getting water out of the little fridge in the room. He turned around and threw one at me. I caught it, but I looked at him with amusement.

"Why the extra hardness?"

Andy's face sobered "don't play with Sarah's emotions Lavonna, I love you like a sister, but Sarah doesn't need someone that just wants certain things from her, she is not a toy."

I flopped into the chair and drank the water down before I responded, trying to reel in my anger because he was only trying to take care of Sarah.

I looked at Andy and asked, "how could you say that? And to be honest I am in love with her and I want to marry Sarah."

Andy looked shocked and regained himself. He ran over, pulled me up and hugged me.

"I am so excited y'all are so cute together. The two people I love the most and Ms. Lavonna Black is off the market. I thought I would never see the day."

I laughed and hugged him back. Well, let me go check on my future wife.

"What are you going to do about Jade?"

Andy asked as I was about to open the door. The happy feeling just seeped out because I was struggling with telling Sarah or just handling it and her never knowing.

"She deserves to know Lavonna." Andy said as I was walking out the door.

I walked to our room and stopped outside the door. Our room sounded so good to me and made me feel warm inside. I opened the door slowly and saw the candles that were still burning but other than that everything was still. I saw that Sarah was asleep on the bed. I walked over to the bed, and I stopped in my tracks. She was so beautiful she was wearing the black satin nightgown, and she had tried to wait up for me as she was reading and fell asleep. I took the book out of her hands and sat it on the nightstand. Covering her up, kissed her on the forehead, and whispered in her ear,

"You will always be my little dragonfly, and I will love you till my dying breath."

I needed to get changed to see little Ms. Jade. I went in the bathroom and changed into some clothes that I didn't care about getting blood on. I would be burning them in the incinerator anyway. I made sure Sarah was still fast asleep and gave her one more kiss on her forehead and eased out of the door.

I walked down to the basement and Jade started screaming at me when I walked in. "Well, it seems like you are stronger than I thought. It is nice to know that you are not broken yet." I said, walking further into the room.

"Just fucking kill me already," she screamed.

"Well, you see Jade I am not ready to snuff out your life just yet. You see I am kind of in a conundrum. I can talk to you right; we are on talking terms."

I pulled her into her nightly chair and strapped her down.

"What should I do, should I tell Sarah about you or should I just take care of you myself." I asked.

"You think that if you tell Sarah she will stay with you after that" she spat at me.

"Humm," I stood there with my chin in my hand thinking you could be right, or you could be wrong. I strolled over to the wall and got the ball gag and gagged Jade.

"I think this is so much better your voice is really grating on my nerves."

I had Leon set up everything for me tonight. I walked over to the table, and everything was sitting there ready for use. I picked up the set of needles and walked back over to Jade. There was a set of twenty. One needle per finger and one for every toe.

I leaned down and slid the first one underneath her fingernail, she screamed and thrashed.

"Stay still, or I may miss and hurt you even more and we would hate that wouldn't we?" I asked.

I moved on to the next nine fingers and after I was done with all ten, I stepped back and admired my handiwork.

"Yesss, I believe we will leave it like this for the first round."

Blood was dripping from all of Jade's fingers while I pulled the cart close to her. I started clamping the wires to each needle.

"This is my first-time using electricity so it may take me a couple of tries to get things right." I said.

Jade was trying to say something, but I ignored her cries. I turned to the machine and cycled it on. Placing it on the lowest setting seeing how far I can go without her passing out. I want her to feel every pulse. I hit the button and Jade started to convulse and scream or try to scream. I let it go for about five seconds. I know five seconds does not seem to be a lot but while being tortured it can seem like an eternity. I stopped, I wasn't a monster or was I. When being tortured, it breaks them down even more you cater to them giving them false hope.

I walked over and picked up a bottle of water and downed half of it then walked over to Jade and undid her gag. She was panting and slobbering all down her face.

"Do you need some water?" I asked.

"Well then open your mouth" and she did without even a rebuttal.

I poured the water in her mouth, and she choked. I moved back to the cart setting the water bottle on the top.

"I am going to leave the gag off."

Jade looked up and something caught her attention. I was about to turn around when Jade screamed with her voice hoarse.

"Sarah, you see what Lavonna has done to me. Do you?...... fucking save me. Princess, you used to love me didn't you please do something." Jade screamed with her voice cracking with emotion.

Chapter 25(Sarah)

Damn, I had fallen asleep waiting for Lavonna to get back. I was wondering what was keeping her out so late every night. I woke up when she was closing the door to the bedroom. I jumped out of bed and almost fell. I stood still seeing if I had made too much noise. Grabbing my robe and headed to the door, I opened the door and was so glad the door was not creaky there. I could see Lavonna walking down a hall. I looked and the house was quiet.

I looked at Andy's room since he was staying here ever since the Jade incident, and it was dark. I hurriedly went after Lavonna because I did not want to lose her. She headed to her study, she was just busy with work, but something was concerning. I watched her enter her study. Should I go in or open the door? I was overrun with anxiety.

Screw it I needed answers and tonight she was going to give them to me.

I slowly opened the door, and I saw Lavonna with her back turned to me. I was about to announce my presence because I thought she was just looking at the books in front of her when she moved the snake bookend, and the door opened inward.

I stilled and a cold shiver ran through my body.

Do not jump to conclusions Sarah.

I scolded myself because I did that often. I was a little bit of an overthinker with a vivid imagination. We are in the BDSM lifestyle, so it is common to have a playroom or a dungeon. Lavonna sure had enough money to have one built but, if that is the case my heart sank.

Could she be entertaining other women?

The thoughts were swirling through my head because I didn't know what to do at this point.

I do not think Andy would have led me into the belly of the beast intentionally. What to do, I paced back in forth in front of the bookshelf.

What have I gotten myself into?

I stopped and closed my eyes and breathed in and out. I am done living my life in fear or running away; that stopped with Jade. I pulled the snake back like Lavonna had and the door opened. There was a winding staircase that went down. I stepped in and the door closed behind me. Well, no going back now, I gotta face Lavonna head on. I made my way down the staircase, the stone beneath my feet felt as cold as ice.

Why didn't I grab my slippers?

The lower I got I heard Lavonna's voice it was a murmur at first but the more I walked down there was so much anger in her voice. I finally made it to the door and the door was ajar a little bit. I was glad it was because I noticed a keypad on the outside. I put my hands on the door and peaked in, I was so scared of what I was going to see.

I looked and saw Jade being tied to a chair. I put both of my hands to my mouth to keep my gasp in. My breathing increased and I thought I was going to hyperventilate. Once I calmed down, I heard Jades screams and I looked through the door again I couldn't really tell everything that was going on. I saw Lavonna was bent down in front of Jade doing something and whatever she was doing Jade was screaming in pain. For a split second I felt satisfaction and then shocked at myself how could I feel this way. Lavonna was torturing Jade and the more I thought about it I knew I should be repulsed and run for safety, but I wasn't, and I felt a little curiosity this must have been where Lavonna was every night before coming to bed.

This is the reason why Andy and Lavonna kept changing the subject about Jade. Andy had to know about this. I watched through the door for a little bit more Lavonna stepped back and walked over to a cart that had a machine on it and I strained to see what Lavonna had done seeing blood flowing from Jades's fingers and then Lavonna started applying wires to something sticking out of Jades fingers then I saw the needles.

Lavonna stepped back and turned on the machine and listened to Jade's screams over and over again. She was so calm, cool, and collected. It was like I was drawn to her. I must have stepped into the room without noticing it because that is when I heard Jades' voice.

"Sarah, you see what Lavonna has done to me. Do you?...... fucking save me. Princess, you used to love me didn't you please do something." she screamed at me.

Bringing my attention back to the room around us. Yep, of course I was standing in the doorway with a long black satin nightgown that hugged all my curves, and the Satin robe hung off one shoulder with no shoes. I looked like a wild woman. I watched as Lavonna turned around and was looking at me up and down, she started walking toward me and it was like I was frozen in one spot. She is in front of me, and I am looking at the ground. She places her finger on my chin and lifts my head.

"Look at me my love."

I am staring into her eyes. Jade starts screaming at me. I go to turn my head and Lavonna still has my chin in her hands.

"Uh Uh sweetness look at me and no one else."

I swallowed so hard it was like my mouth was suddenly dry and I opened my mouth to speak but, nothing came out.

"Yes, sweetness what do you want to say you have the floor first." Lavonna said.

I straightened myself and looked her in the eyes with determination.

"I need an explanation."

I was so proud of myself because even though I was a wreck inside my voice came out steady and firm.

A smile curved her lips and said,

"Good girl never be afraid to communicate anything to me."

She dropped her hand and stepped aside and let me take in the room.

"This was and is me sweetness this is where my deepest darkest secrets hide. I am someone people call to handle things that they don't or can't handle."

Lavonna held out her hand and waited for me to take it. I did even though all of this was overwhelming. I felt safe with Lavonna safer than I have ever felt in my life.

Was I the crazy one here?

She led me around the room, and we ended up in front of Jade. Jade had tears streaming down her face. Multiple cuts from her face all the way down her body. As I stared at Jade, I felt nothing. I don't know if it was shock or just realizing I was okay with this and maybe feeling guilty but not in the normal way. Guilt, that this did not bother me. Maybe I had been a little crazy in the end.

I looked at Lavonna and she was standing off to the side watching me.

"If you cannot handle all of this and do not want to be with me anymore that is ok you can walk out of that door and Andy will take you home but know after tonight you will never have to worry about Jade anymore and you can live your life in peace."

I looked at her and then looked at Jade and when I looked at Jade anger flared for what she had done to me. Jade had broken me but not only physically she broke me mentally to control me. Years of abuse came flashing back. It didn't happen overnight but all of it came rushing back to me. Lavonna slowly walked into the light. I saw she had a thigh sheath on and there was a knife sitting in it. I turned to her and kissed her hard and took the knife out of the sheath and before I could stop myself, I slit Jade's throat, and I stood in front of Jade watching the life drain out of her eyes and my eyes blurring over and I realized it was tears blurring my vision.

I was still standing there holding the blade in my hand blood dripping from it onto the floor and something warm started flowing around my feet. Staring down Jades' blood was running around my feet. Lavonna came to me and talked to me slowly.

"Baby, give me the knife."

I let her take it from my hand and heard it clank on the floor somewhere out of reach probably. She pulled me into an embrace, us both standing while Jade's blood ran all around us. I stared into Lavonna's eyes.

"It is all over now. No more running" I spoke out loud.

I felt Lavonna's arms close around me as my world started to darken but even in the darkness all I could feel was peace.

Epilogue

A couple months later my body healed the bruises and everything but, I have to say I have a really good Doctor/Nurse. Doctor when she wanted to be stern and complain about me doing anything and Nurse when she wanted to be sweet and tend to me. Anyway, tonight is date night, and I am so excited. My hair is curled my makeup flawless and heels to top off and put sexy in sexiness. I looked in the mirror and it looked like I was glowing. My phone started to ring and from the ringtone I could tell it was Lavonna. I ran to get it off the bedside table and answered my breathing was a little erratic and I said *hello* she started giggling her voice got me every time making my thighs clinch.

"Why are you out of breath I can give you something to be out of breath about. Are you ready sweetness your chariot awaits you outside."

"I am on my way my love." I said.

I grabbed my purse and headed out to the front and as I was walking down the stairs Lavonna was standing there looking like someone that had just walked out of a magazine. She was gorgeous but gorgeous in a way that she commanded the room around her. The suit she wore was tailored to her and I could feel the wetness between my legs. I should have worn underwear because every time I was even around her, I was a dripping mess. Screw it I walked down the stairs and Lavonna's eyes followed me down to her. She kissed me,

"You look good enough to devour sweetness cannot wait till I get you out of that gorgeous dress of yours. You are mine forever and always."

She grabbed my hand, and we walked outside to the black limo waiting for us Leon was the driver tonight.

"Good evening, Leon how the wife and kids?" I ask.

"They are great Ms. Lively thank you for asking."

Lavonna whispered in my ear "Do you trust me?"

I nodded, she pulled a blindfold out and placed it over my eyes. She led me into the limo. I was excited and bummed, this was my first time in a limo, and I could not see anything but darkness. I heard Lavonna slipping out of her jacket and then she kissed me as I kissed her back. She pulled away.

"Baby I want you right now I can't wait you look devine."

She leaned into my ear and whispered, "sit back and enjoy the ride."

She was in between my legs, her hands trailing up my legs pulling up my dress we don't want to mess up this gorgeous dress. She kissed me again. My pussy ached for her touch. Her fingers found my pussy and rubbed.

"Oooo you are always so wet and ready I love it."

She plunged her fingers inside me, I gasped she added another finger and pushed in and out of me. I felt her breathe along my thigh. While she had her fingers buried deep inside of me her mouth devoured my clit playing and teasing it not pushing me to the edge just teasing then her tongue licked that spot and I grabbed both sides of the seat I braced myself as her fingers moved in and out of me and her tongue playing with my clit she focused on that spot and I was almost bursting when she thrust her fingers deep as they could go and brought me over the edge. I screamed her name riding the waves of pleasure.

"Let me clean you up baby."

Lavonna was there with something warm and cleaned me up. At that moment when I was cleaned up and she pulled my dress back down. Leon came over the speaker.

"We have arrived Ms. Black."

Lavonna grabbed my hand and asked if I wanted to go for a walk.

"Well, it looks like I don't have any other choice, do I?" I replied with a smile.

"You always have a choice my Lil dragonfly."

I got out and I heard the waves, and the smell of ocean hit my nose. We were at the beach but why did I think we were going out tonight? She walked me a few yards.

"Sit down"

I did, and she was at my feet taking my heels off "we will need these later."

She grabbed my hand, and my toes hit the sand. I love walking on the beach, it calmed me so much. I could hear the seagulls in the distance and hear the waves coming closer and closer, then I felt the warm water run over my feet. We walked a little in the water and finally stopped.

"Close your eyes baby and let me take the blindfold off."

I did as she asked.

"Open your eyes."

I slowly opened my eyes and Lavonna was on one knee in front of me holding out a ring. There were candles all around us. The sun was setting, and the sky was an array of oranges and pinks, it was beautiful. I looked at Lavonna and she was smiling ear to ear.

"Sarah Lively my little snake doctor the one that loves all parts of me will you become mine forever?"

Tears slipped down my face.

"Yes, my love, I want to be yours forever." I replied jumping up and down in the sand.

She placed the ring on my finger and kissed me like she would never get another one. She looked at me.

"To a lifetime of Dark Desires being fulfilled and till death do us part."

EVEN VILLAINS LIVE HAPPILY EVERAFTER

9 798330 657049